His sex kitten

By

Jane Ashton

Table of content

Chapter 1

Neil was in his office sitting behind his desk looking up sites that sell kittens, he wanted to surprise his niece by getting her a pet for her birthday. Only what popped up was not with animals, but with women. Just then his friend Eric Hopkins walked in and went over to him, looking over his shoulder.

"Wow, what do we have here?" he asked, looking at the women on the screen.

"I'm not sure. I was looking for kittens for sale and this came up."

Eric read what it said out loud. "Kittens for rent, by day, week or month. Willing to do whatever you want, for parties, personal use or just to have some fun. I don't think your sister will appreciate you giving your five-year-old niece one of these," he said laughing.

"So what is this site, is it a dating site or a prostitute one?" Neil asked as he scrolled down at the different women on the page.

"I have heard of it, I think it's a dating site only it's more to do with getting laid. This might be good for you, you wouldn't have to worry about these women looking for a ring. Scroll down some more, let's see what they have." After five minutes Eric told him to stop and pointed to a young blond. "Damn, she's hot."

Neil stared at the woman on the screen, she was drop-dead gorgeous. Blond hair, a great figure and it was her eyes that drew him in. They were big and emerald green, but he could see the sadness in them. "She looks so young," he said, rubbing his chin.

"It says all the women are twenty-one and older," Eric replied. "Hey, are you thinking of renting a woman, isn't that kind of sleazy?"

"I do need to get laid soon and I am going away for a couple of weeks. It would be nice to take someone with me and get regular sex. I don't feel like going through the whole wining and dining thing just to end up going to bed alone. I'm going for it Eric, this is the woman I'm bidding on, she's beautiful." He clicked on her picture and placed his bid, making it high to ensure he'd get her. He had to state he wanted her for one month and put down an amount that would choke a horse.

"You better not let your sister know about this or she'll never let you anywhere near your niece again."

"Well I'm not going to tell her, and don't you breathe a word to her or our friendship is over, you got that?"

"Judy won't hear it from me, as long as you take me out to lunch," he said, giving Neil a punch in the arm.

He did take his friend to lunch then after making sure his business was running smoothly he went up to the penthouse suite of his hotel. After showering he logged on to his computer and checked his messages. There was one from the sex kitten site. He smiled when he saw that his bid was the highest and was asked to put in his information and was asked to send payment to a bank account. Once they received payment the girl would be brought to the place of his choice when he was ready.

Once he did it he went to his bedroom and looked into the full-length mirror. He was proud of his looks, he was tall and fit and he never had trouble getting women. Then he looked down at his manhood, he knew the women loved how well-endowed he was. All the men in his family were blessed in that department and what made it better was he knew how to work it.

The following day he found a shelter that had dogs and kittens. He found a black and white one that he thought was friendly so he bought it for his niece and headed over to his sister's place to give it to her. He had also bought a carrier, cat litter, and everything she would need for it. When he arrived the little girl, Chrissy jumped up and down, giving him hugs and kisses.

Judy stood with her arms crossed as the kids ran around, snacks and birthday cakes were already placed on the counter. "You just had to get her a kitten didn't you?"

He stood back, leaning against the counter. "I could have got her a puppy, maybe next year," he said, laughing when he saw the look of horror that crossed her face.

"Don't you dare," she said, slapping his arm. "Go in the other room with the men and have a beer, unless you want to entertain the kids." She shook her head when he took off. "Coward," she shouted behind his back.

It was close to midnight, the kids were long tucked into bed and the grownups had a few beers and played some poker.

"So are you ever going to settle down?" Judy's husband Roy asked Neil.

"Now why would I want to do that when there are so many ladies out there? I can't deprive them of all of this," he said, grabbing his crotch, making the men laugh and the women shake their heads in disgust.

"One of these days you are going to meet a woman that will change your mind," Judy said, giving him the snake eye. "When you do you'll forget about other women and then, just maybe you'll be happy."

"I'm happy now," he said, turning serious.

She went and sat next to him, placing her hand under his chin. "No, you're not, not really. You haven't been happy since you took over your father's business when he passed away. Now you have all those fake women chasing after you, you go from one woman to another to hide the fact that you're lonely. Find the right one brother and you'll never be sad or lonely again."

"You're talking nonsense sister, I'm happy the way things are. I have to go now but this was fun, next is a puppy," he said, giving her a kiss on the cheek he left to go home. Judy was always trying to get him to settle down, she even tried to fix him up with some of her friends, which he found to be plain and dull.

He went home and took a beer from the fridge and sat down with his laptop. He opened up the Sex Kitten site and took another look at her picture. He couldn't stop looking at her eyes, they were so beautiful and he couldn't wait until the following Friday when she came to his place. He wondered what it would be like to sleep with her, to make love to her whenever and wherever he wanted.

The closer it came to the day she would be arriving the more excited he became. He had the fridge stocked with food, and he went and bought some condoms. He was having a hard time keeping his mind on work.

Eric showed up at his suite the night she was to show up, staying for a couple of drinks. "So when is she getting here?" he asked, looking at his watch. He was curious to see her, thinking maybe he should call the site and get himself a sex kitten.

"You'll be long gone before she gets here," he answered.

"Well, you're no fun. You ought to let me meet her, check her out for you and if you don't like her I can take the girl off your hands."

"You're one sick fucker Eric, now finish your drink and beat it."

Later he changed into sweatpants and a tee shirt and he heard someone knocking at the door. He went and opened it and when he did he first noticed the man with his hand around the woman's arm. He wore a suit, and was a big brute of a guy, he then looked at the blond who appeared a little afraid and she wasn't looking back at him. She really was gorgeous, she wore a short black dress and heels and her long hair hung down past her shoulders.

"You Neil Hicks?" he asked, looking him up and down.

"Yeah, that's me."

"I'm here with your kitten," he said, letting go of her until he reached into his jacket and pulled out a form. "Just sign here," he points to the checkmark.

He took the form and signed it, handing it back to the man.

"Thank you, I'll be back for her in a month, enjoy." He then set her suitcase down and walked away.

He picked up her case and stepped back. "Come in, make yourself at home." He waited until she was in then closed the door. "So what's your name?"

"Kitten," she replied as she looked around the room. She had only seen places like this in books and magazines, she had to wonder what he did for a living and how rich he was. But she knew better than to ask questions, the last time she did she was black and blue for a week.

"No, your real name."

"Kitten, just Kitten," she answered back to him.

"OK, have it your way, Kitten. I'll just put your things in my room and when I get back we can get acquainted. Please, have a seat, I'll just be a minute." Taking her bag he carried it into the other room. She was not what he was expecting, he was expecting someone more talkative, bold, and brazen. But this woman was quiet and shy and he could tell she was nervous which had him thinking she was new to this job.

He came out and over to where she was sitting. "Can I get you something to drink?"

"I'll have whatever you're having," she answered quietly.

He poured them both a scotch on the rocks and handed her one, he then sat down next to her and watched her take a sip. She started choking and her eyes watered up. It was obvious to him that she wasn't used to drinking the hard stuff. He takes the glass from her and stands up. "I think you'd be happier with a glass of wine." He comes back with the white wine and sits back down.

"Thank you," she said, taking it from him.

"As you know I'm Neil Hicks and you'll be here with me for a month. I expect you to go with me to certain functions and we'll be going to Italy for a couple of weeks. Have you ever been there?"

She shakes her head and takes a drink of her wine.

"You'll love it, it's one of the most beautiful and romantic places in the world. I own this hotel and casino. I don't want you to get the idea that this arrangement of ours is going to turn into something more permanent. I also expect you to act like a lady around other people and not flirt with another man. After all, you're here for me, just me. Look at me," he said and waited for her to turn and look at him. "Have I made myself clear?"

"Yes," she answered.

"Now tell me something about you."

"What do you want to know?"
"Your real name for one."
"I'm not supposed to tell."
"Why not?"
"It's against the rules."
He pinches the bridge of his nose. "I don't give a damn about the rules. We will be around family and friends and I can't introduce you as a Kitten."
"Kiara Finn."
"How old are you?"
"Twenty-two," she said, finishing her wine in one gulp.
Taking the glass from her hand he went and poured her another wine. "Here, you look like you could use another." He sits back down. "How long have you been doing this job?"
"Not long."
"You don't give out much information, do you? and don't say it's against the rules. Now I'll only ask you one more time, how long have you been in this business and how many clients have you had?"
"Like I said, not long and you are my first client."
"So that's why you look so scared. I want you to know I won't hurt you, I only want consensual sex and a companion when I go to Italy. Are you up for that or would you like to call this off? I could call the site and tell them I changed my mind."
"No, please don't call them. I'm just a little nervous but I'm up to this, I'll do whatever you want."
He saw the look of fear in her eyes, and wondered why, what was she afraid of? But he chalked it up to her being new to the business. "OK, so how

does this work, where do we start?" he asked, watching her as she took another long drink of her wine.

Putting her glass down she lifted her dress up and straddled him. Her lips went to his neck and she started kissing as she spoke. "We can start however you want to. I can get on my knees and give you a blow job or we can go right to bed and there you can do anything you want to." She felt his cock getting hard against her as she kissed his neck. Though he was handsome and smelled amazing she still felt dirty. She wanted to run out screaming but her life was in danger if she tried to get away. It could be worse, he could have been an old creep who would abuse her. She didn't know this Neil but she felt he wasn't a sick pervert or abusive, at least that's what she was hoping.

He closed his eyes when she sucked gently on his neck, it felt so good. "You are on the pill right?" he asked, causing her to stop.

She stopped to look at him, feeling his cock pressing against her. "Yes, but you know the rules, you have to wear a condom every time."

He brushed the hair from her face. "I always do, but it never hurts for you to be on the pill. Better safe than sorry." He shifted her so that she was laying flat on her back, him on top of her." A blow job sounds good, but another time. Let's just slow down a little. Are you hungry?"

His offering her food when he was clearly turned on confused her. "I am but don't you want sex first?"
"We have lots of time for that, right now I need something to eat. I'll order something from downstairs and have them send it up." He gets off her and reaches for his phone. "Is there anything you're in the mood for?"
She sat up, adjusting her dress. "Anything is fine with me."
He ordered them a shrimp salad and pasta. "If you'd like to go put your things away I emptied a drawer for you and a space in the closet.'
"Alright, thanks," she said, getting up and going in the direction he pointed to. Going to his room she looked around. The bed was what caught her eye first, It was huge, and she swallowed what felt like a giant lump in her throat. It was just a matter of time before she would have to perform whatever acts of sex that he wanted. She was scared as hell, she'd only had sex a few times with her boyfriend, or ex-boyfriend and that was over a year ago. After putting her things away she goes back into the other room just as the food arrives.
During the meal he made small talk, trying to put her at ease. When she got up and went to tidy up he took her hand. "It can wait, come with me."
This was it she thought as he led her into the bedroom. She shivered when they got there and he shut the door, his hand going to the back of her neck he drew her close, his lips going to her neck where he started kissing softly. She closed her

eyes, she didn't want to enjoy it but it did feel so good and she let out a small moan.

Hearing her moan he got excited, there was nothing like the sound of a woman moaning in pleasure. He stopped and stepped back, his hands going to the hem of her dress he pulled it up over her head. He looked down at her breasts that were barely covered by the skimpy bra she had on, it was red and she wore matching panties. "Beautiful, so beautiful," he said and reaching behind her unhooked her bra and let it fall to the floor. Taking a breast in each hand he began caressing them, his cock growing hard, straining against his pants. Hands moving down to her hips he put his fingers in the waistband of the panties and pulled them down as he squatted. His face was level with her pussy so pushing her closer he buried his face in it. She was clean shaved and he left some kisses before getting to his feet.

She started breathing heavily, her core was throbbing and she could feel the wetness pooling between her legs. When he started unbuttoning his shirt and sliding it off she started yanking his sweats down. Her hand wrapped around his shaft and she moved her hand slowly up and down, feeling it throbbing. Figuring he wanted a blow job she gets down on her knees and takes him in her mouth. She heard him grunting, his breathing becoming ragged as his fingers raked through her hair.

When she started gagging he stopped her, pulling her up so that she was face-to-face with him. "Get on the bed," he ordered her and reached for a condom from off the dresser. As he rolled it over him he kept his eyes on her. His eyes moved up and down her body when she lay down, her eyes closing. Getting into the bed he climbed on top of her, his lips going to hers he started kissing her. His hand moved down between her legs and he felt how wet she was. Then he grabbed his cock and slowly entered her, feeling her gasp as her arms went around him.

"Shit, you're so wet, so tight," he said between kissing her. He had never felt this much heat or tightness around his cock before and it felt amazing, getting him hornier which caused him to start thrusting harder and faster into her. He was so close to coming and normally he would have been with any other woman but for some reason he wanted her to come first, to experience pleasure first. It wasn't long before he knew she was close but she was holding back, she seemed to be fighting it. "Come for me, let me hear your pleasure."

His body was so toned and rock hard, he had a six-pack and a perfect v-line going down and he was well endowed, too much for her small mouth. His touch and kiss sent a heat wave coursing through her body. First, she tried to make her mind go blank, not wanting to enjoy it but the more he moved and caressed her body she found herself coming alive from his touch. Then when he told her to come she did just that. She cried out oh God as she started squirming frantically beneath him, her nails scraping down his back as she exploded with what she assumed was an orgasm, as she had never experienced one before. She thought it was over but then he started pounding into her, grunting and moaning as he came, bringing her to another orgasm before he collapsed on top of her.

He lifted himself up, hovering over her. “I think this month is going to be great and we'll be having a lot more fun like this," he said, giving her a kiss. Getting off her he walks into the bathroom and flushes the condom. "I'm getting something to drink, would you like one?" he asked, pulling on his sweats.

"Water please," she answered, pulling the covers over her.

He came back with water for her and juice for him and got back into bed. "You really are beautiful," he said, pushing her hair back. "I'm so glad I came across that site and saw your picture."

"So you haven't been on it before?" she asked, hoping he wouldn't get mad.

He chuckled and laid back, putting his hands behind his head. "No. I was actually looking for kittens for sale, I wanted to get one for my niece for her birthday. Instead, I stumbled across this site, and at first, I was shocked and then curious. It's late, we should get some sleep. I hope you're not a cuddler, I really like my space and can't sleep with a woman in my arms."

"No, I'm not," she said, moving over to the other end of the bed.

"I didn't mean for you to move so far away, you can lay next to me." He smiled when she moved back over and rolled onto her side, her back to him. "I like that you have no hair down there, so soft and I like not getting any pubic hair in my mouth."

She closed her eyes, her body tensing up, was he planning on putting his mouth down there again, and if so exactly what was he planning on doing? She had heard stories of how a man would put their tongue inside them but she never had it done to her and wasn't sure if she'd like it. But if that's what he wanted to do to her she had no choice but to let him and she would pretend to like it.

He leaned over to kiss her cheek. "Night," he said, and rolling onto his side he went to sleep, feeling satisfied.

She lay there awake long after he had fallen asleep, listening to him breathing. Turning around onto her side she watches him. She found it strange that a man that looks the way he does would need to go on a sex site to get a woman. Surely he had women throwing themselves at him. It came as a surprise to hear that they were going to Italy. Which was maybe a good thing, it could be the perfect opportunity for her to run away and they would never find her there.

Neil woke up first and went to take a shower and when he came out she was not in bed so putting on a pair of pants he went to see where she had gotten to. He found her in the kitchen, making breakfast. This made him smile, it was good to know that she could cook and wasn't expecting room service every time she was with him.

She knew he was there, but after what they had done in his bed last night she felt a little shy, not wanting to look at him. "I hope you don't mind that I made us breakfast, I wasn't sure what you liked so I went ahead and made french toast and bacon."

"I don't mind, I'm actually quite pleased, thanks," he said and sat down at the table. "I see you're wearing one of my shirts, don't you have a nightgown?"

Thinking he was angry at her for wearing it she was afraid that he would punish her and she started to shake. "I'm sorry, I'll go take it off."

He grabbed her arm before she could walk away. "No, it's alright, really. I was just wondering if you brought any nightgowns with you." He was shocked to see how afraid she was and the way her body trembled.

She lowered her head when he pulled her down on his lap. "I don't have any. I usually just sleep in my panties and a t-shirt."

"I noticed you didn't have much in the way of clothes so we'll go shopping and get you a few things, some sexy nighties too while we're at it." He ran his hand over her leg but stopped when he felt her body tensing up and she squeezed her legs together. It would appear his little kitten still hadn't warmed up completely to him.

"You shouldn't be buying me clothes."

"We're going to Italy, you will need some decent clothes to wear, and a couple of evening dresses for when we go dancing and to the opera."

"Opera?" she asked, looking at him.

"I'll take you if you've never been to one."

"No, I haven't."

"I think you'll like it, now dish out my food, I'm starving."

Getting off his lap she goes over to the counter and makes him up a plate, and one for her. At first, she thought he was going to get mad when he touched her legs and she tensed up but he didn't seem to be so she was able to relax.

When they were done eating he pushed his plate away. "That was really good, thank you. I'll wash up if you would like to take a shower and then we'll hit the shops. I want you to get whatever you want and will need for our trip."

"When are we going and for how long?"

"The middle of next week and we'll be staying for two weeks. Is something wrong?" he asked when he saw she looked worried.

"I don't have a passport."

He rubbed his chin and thought about it for a minute. "I know some people, I'll get you one in no time." When she went to shower he did up the dishes and made a call to his buddy, asking for a favor. "Thanks, you can get it to me before we leave, right?" Hanging up he sat down and waited for her to come out. He knew she was new to this job but he got the impression there was more to this woman than she was letting on. He hoped that in time he would be able to get her to open up and tell him more about herself.

Chapter 2

When she came out she had on a black skirt with a white blouse, he waited for her to put her shoes on and then they left his suite. "I need to stop downstairs at my office and sign some papers then we'll be on our way." Though it was Saturday, he wanted to get it over with so that he wouldn't have to be bothered on Monday. With his hand on the small of her back, he led her to the elevator and they got in.

"You have an office here?" she asked, looking around as they walked past the desk and the casino. the front

"Yes, I own this place," he said and steered her into his office. He motioned for her to sit down while he pulled out some papers and signed them. Putting them away he got up and they left the building. “There are some great shops here on the strip so we can just walk."

They walked into one of the best shops on the strip and Neil instructed the saleswomen to show them some dresses and other clothing. For three hours she tried on different outfits, he wanted to see her in them. Since she wasn't giving him an idea of what she liked he went ahead and chose for her. He paid for the items and told the saleswoman to have them delivered too. He also made sure she got new bras and panties and some sexy lingerie.

"You really shouldn't have bought so much," she said, feeling guilty.

"You needed them.," he answered, smiling.

"But they were so expensive, haven't you spent enough money renting me?" She stopped talking when she saw the angry look that crossed his face. Oh, she knew she should have kept her mouth shut.

He stopped talking, his temper flared up, and grabbing her by the shoulders he put her up against the wall. "I don't want you saying that ever again, it makes you sound like a whore and me a sick pervert."

"I'm sorry," she said, lowering her head and she felt the tears spring to her eyes. "But isn't that what I am?"

Releasing her shoulders, his temper disappearing, he used his finger under her chin to lift her head up so that he could look into her eyes. "You're not a whore, never say that again." He felt his heart melt when he saw she was close to tears. "Would you like to walk some more or are you tired?"

"We can walk some more," she answered. She was surprised when he took her hand and held it as they walked further down the strip.

He stopped to look at her. "How would you like to go see the Titanic artifact exhibition?"

"Sure, that sounds like fun," she said, only having heard about it she was excited. She looked around in awe when they got there. "This is amazing. I've watched all the movies they made of it, the old and the new ones. It's so sad that all those people lost their lives."

He leaned over the railing, looking at the display. "My great-grandparents were on that boat when it went down, they never made it."
"I'm so sorry," she said, turning to look at him.
"It's alright, I never knew them. Come, let's see the rest of it." Taking her hand again they continued walking, stopping to look at the photos of all the ones who were on it when it went down.
By the time they were finished, it was dinner time so they stopped at one of the restaurants to grab a bite to eat.
"So tell me Kiara, are your parents alive?"
"Are you?" she asked, trying to steer him away from asking about her.
"Why do you do that?" he asked, staring back at her.
"Do what?"
"Avoiding my questions by asking ones of your own."
She set her fork down. "We're not allowed to talk about ourselves, it makes things too personal so please don't ask me any more questions."
"Alright. My parents died a few years back, there's just me and my sister Judy. She's married and has a little girl, Chrissy. She's cute as a button, she's who I bought a kitten for. We are having dinner with them Wednesday night, the night before we leave for Italy."
"You want me to meet your family?"
"My sister is always trying to set me up with her friends, this way if I let her think you're my girlfriend

she'll stop. So will you go along with it, help me out?"

"I'm here to do whatever you want so yes."

He paid the bill and they went back to his hotel. He followed her into the kitchen when she said she was going to get a glass of water. He stood with his arms crossed and watched as she tipped the glass up to her lips and drank. His sexual urges rose so going over he takes the glass out of her hand and sets it down. He then lifts her up onto the counter, letting his hands slide up her legs.

His mouth came down on hers, his kiss turned hot and passionate as his hand slid up her dress and between her legs, rubbing her pussy over the material of her panties. He stopped kissing her, knocking everything off the counter he put his hand on her chest and lightly pushed her down. He pulled off her panties and spreading her legs he put his mouth against her sex. He licked and sucked until he heard her scream and she came, her orgasm making her body tremble.

Wiping his mouth he picked her up and carried her to the bedroom where he laid her down, tearing off the rest of her clothes. Getting up he quickly shed his own clothes and put a condom over his throbbing erection. He thrust his cock inside her, going in hard and deep, making her gasp. He was so aroused he didn't take his time, he pounded into her hard until they both came.

She was a little shocked at the force of his lovemaking, it was so intense. The first time he made sure she was satisfied before he was, this time he acted like he didn't care, and just when she thought he was going to treat her right, she felt hurt. Not wanting to anger him she put her arms around him, kissing him back. Then he said something that made her feel just a little better.

"I'm so sorry, I was just so turned on by you that I lost control. I'm sorry if I was rough and didn't take my time. I promise it won't happen again."

She thought back to when they were in the kitchen and what he did to her, it was amazing, drove her mad with desire when his tongue played inside her, the way he sucked, pulling on her clit and bringing her to the best orgasm ever. She figured since he gave her so much pleasure and she must have gotten him so aroused with her screams and the way she moaned that he lost control, so yes, she would forgive him.

"That's alright, it did scare me a little at first but then it was amazing." She pulled his head down to kiss him. This was something she never thought she would do, to kiss him without being made to feel as if she had to.

"No, it's not alright, shit I never gave you time before I entered it into you." He pulled her into his arms, stroking her back. "I'm sorry," he said, kissing the top of her head. He lay there a while before getting up to dispose of the condom. When he came back to bed she was asleep so he got in, lay on his side and watched her until he fell asleep.

"Morning sleepyhead," he said to her when she walked into the kitchen. "I thought you were going to sleep all day," he said, handing her a mug of steaming hot coffee.

Her brows drew together and she bit her lower lip. "I'm sorry," she said, apologizing.

"Kiara, it's alright, don't look so worried, I was just kidding with you," he said when he saw how scared she was. He moved closer, touching her cheek with the palm of his hand. "I hope that soon you'll open up and tell me what is making you scared."

She looked into his eyes and saw concern, he was nothing like what she had heard some of the clients were like. Unlike the other men, Neil was kind, gentle, and maybe a little bossy but still appeared to be a good guy. "It's nothing really, thanks for the coffee. Would you like me to make you something to eat?"

"No, that's alright. I have some business to take care of downstairs but you go ahead and make something for yourself. I have a surprise for you this afternoon."

"A surprise, what kind of surprise?"

"I'm taking you on a tour of Las Vegas, by helicopter."

"I've never been on one before, is it safe?" she asked, feeling nervous.

"Yes, it's perfectly safe, you have nothing to worry about," he said before leaving to get some work done. He didn't want to leave her but he still had a business to run.

She was wearing jeans and a black top when he came back four hours later, she noticed he was in a bad mood. "Are you sure you want to take me out? We could just stay here and I'll make dinner."

"Why?" he said, sitting down and rubbing the back of his neck.

"You look angry so I just thought we should stay in."

"I am pissed, pissed at my staff. Look, there was a major screw up but I took care of it and I already booked the helicopter so we're going," he snapped. Feeling bad about snapping at her he smiled at her. "Getting away from here and having some fun will make me feel better. Just let me change my clothes and we'll be on our way."

Leaving the hotel they went to the indoor parking lot and he opened the door to his BMW and waited until she was seated before going around to the driver's side. He was feeling a little more human after having a long hot shower. He did consider having her join him but he knew if she had they wouldn't be leaving the bedroom for the rest of the day.

She was a little nervous about getting into the small helicopter but once they took off she started to enjoy it. Neil would point out certain landmarks, making jokes which had her laughing, something she hadn't done in quite some time.

When they circled back around he pointed. "There's my hotel."

"It looks so beautiful from up here," she stated as she looked down at the bright lights that lit it up.

It was getting dark by the time they landed and were seated inside his car.

"I had fun, thank you, Neil." She looked over at him, wanting to ask him something but wasn't sure if she should.

"Why do I get the feeling that you want to ask me something?" he asked when he saw the way she looked at him. "It's really alright to ask me things."

Taking a deep breath she went for it. "You hired me to be your sex kitten, for sex but yet you take me places, you show me a good time. I thought this was just supposed to be about sex, it feels more like dating."

He placed his hand on her leg, and looking at her he turned serious. "It's not dating, I don't want you to think it is. You are here just to give me sex, but I see no reason why we can't have some fun outside of the bedroom. Now, let's go and get something to eat. I'm thinking of pizza and beer. I know this great bar that makes the best pizza around."

He drove for twenty minutes and stopped outside the bar, going inside he ordered the food and asked her what she wanted to drink. He smiled when she said she also wanted a beer. He was pleased that she could drink something other than wine, except for the hard stuff that he knew she couldn't handle.

He ignored the waitress who was so boldly flirting with him even though he was there with someone. To him, it showed what kind of a woman she was, one who didn't care about the other person he was there with and he found it to be a huge turnoff.

When the music started up again he got up and held out his hand. "Would you like to dance with me?"

She smiled, taking his hand she got up and followed him over to the dance area.

He held her in his arms, she fit so perfectly that it felt so natural having her there. There was something so different about her from the other women he had been with. She was sweet, soft, and held so much mystery, which he planned on finding out about. He liked the way she held him, the way she rested her head on his shoulder.

She looks up at him. “I'm tired, I'd like to go home now, if that's alright?"

His heart melted when she looked at him with those beautiful eyes of hers, she also looked as though she was afraid to ask him if they could leave. "Yes, we can leave now, I'm also very tired, it's been a long day for both of us."

They walked out of the bar and as they were getting into the car two men who were half in the bag came up to them. Neil shook his head, it was the same old cliche, the one where they started saying some unflattering things about the woman, thinking they could take him down and do some unthinkable things to her.

"Come on guys, that's no way to talk to a lady, just go home and sleep it off and I'll let you walk away without any broken bones." The two men were large and he knew they thought because he, himself was smaller, less bulky that he wouldn't stand a chance against them. Little did they know he studied fine art in self-defense with the world's most famous master in karate.

"Just get in your car and leave the girl with us and we won't have a problem," said the bigger one of the two.

He felt her hand on his back and heard her breathing hitching in her throat. The last thing he wanted was for her to witness his violent side, but he might not have a choice. He wasn't about to let these men get their hands on her. "Sorry boys, I can't do that." He turned to her. "Get in the car and lock the doors."

Not wanting to leave him she did what he told her to do and watched from inside as the two men charged at him. All she could see were fists flying, and a lot of kicks and jumps. Neil was like a one-man fighting machine as he took the men down, both of them bleeding and crying out in pain. She saw him taking his phone from his back pocket and making a call. She unlocked the door and stepped out, going over to him she looked at the two men laying on the ground.

"We have to wait for the police to come," he said, wiping the blood from his lip with the back of his hand.

"Where did you learn to fight like that?" she asked, impressed.

"It's a long story, maybe someday I'll tell you."

"I was scared, I thought you were going to kill them."

"I could have, but the thing is what I've learned is to use it only in self-defense, not to kill."

The cops showed up, their statement was taken and the two men were taken into custody. Neil gave them his address and phone number then they were allowed to leave. Knowing she was still shaken up he held her hand all the way back to the hotel.

When they got back to his suite he told her to go ahead and get ready for bed, he wanted a drink before joining her. He needed to unwind, he wanted to kill those men for the things they said they wanted to do to her. It took everything he learned, all the years of training to fight the urge not to end their pathetic lives.

Putting on one of the sexy nightgowns that he bought her she went into the living room, finding him with a drink in his hand, he was staring out the window. Walking over to where he was she put her arms around his waist from behind, resting her cheek against his back. "Why don't you come to bed?" When he turned around to face her she put her arms around his neck, pressing her body up against him, letting him know she wanted him.

"Are you coming on to me?" he asked, feeling the heat inside him rising.

"If I kiss you or suck on your neck will you rip off my nightgown and make love to me?" she asked, running her fingers over the back of his head.

"Maybe. Try it and see what happens," he said, putting his arms around her waist, his cock already hard, wanting her. When she placed her lips softly on his neck and started kissing he closed his eyes, loving the feeling that swept through him. He reached over to touch her breasts and he felt how hard her nipples were.

"Oh Neil," she moaned when his hand moved from one breast to the other, running his thumb over the nipples. He took a fistful of her hair and pulled her head up, his mouth came down hard on hers. She let him dominate her, his tongue forcing its way inside her mouth as his kiss turned more passionate, a little rough, and then she was lifted up into his arms. Making it to the bedroom he put her down where they tore off each other's clothes, falling onto the bed.

He started off by kissing her lips, moving down her neck, his hand wrapped around her breast, and putting it in his mouth. He felt how her back arched when he sucked on the nipple and her fingers gripping his hair. He moved to the other breast before kissing down her stomach and parting her legs. He pleasured her until she cried out his name and she orgasmed. Putting on a condom he entered her wet opening slowly. He made love to her that night three times, it wasn't sex, it was making love, it was warm, gentle, and passionate.

The next day he was taking a shower when there was a knock at the door. She debated whether or not to answer the door but then decided to. It was a man she had never seen before, he was around Neil's age, and almost as good-looking.

"Can I help you?" she asked, stepping back when he walked in.

"I'm here to see Neil."

"He's taking a shower, he should be out any minute."

"You must be Kiara, he's told me about you. I'm his friend, Eric Hopkins and it's a pleasure to meet you."

"Thank you," she said, wondering just how much Neil had told Eric. The last thing she wanted was for people to know what she was doing for a living.

"Can I get you something to drink, coffee or tea?"

"No thanks, I'm good."

Neil came into the room doing up his shirt and saw Eric talking with her. "What brings you here so early?"

"I was in the neighborhood and thought I'd drop in and say hi and meet your friend. I was waiting for you to invite me so when you didn't I decided to pop in on my own," he said and went to sit down on the sofa.

"I'll leave you two alone to talk," she said, moving closer, kissed his cheek, and went back to the bedroom.

"Where's the kitten going?" Eric asked, watching her leave.

"Don't call her that, her name is Kiara," he snapped, glaring at Eric.

"OK, calm down. I didn't mean any harm, don't tell me you're becoming smitten by her. You have to remember that she is really nothing more than a prostitute."

"She's not a prostitute."

"Neil, you paid for her to stay with you for a month to have sex with. She seems sweet and all but taking money for sex does make her one. You can't fall for someone like that, just have your fun with her then cut her loose when the month is up."

"I have no plans on falling for her, but I do like her and I get the feeling she doesn't like this job, that maybe she wants out. I am her first client."

"Oh come on Neil, she probably tells all her clients that."

"No, I believe her."

"What do you know about this girl? She could be a good liar, don't fall for it, she's a pro. When your time is up with her I just might go on the site and book her for a few days."

"I think it's time for you to go," he said, standing up. "Don't even think for one minute that you'll get her." It pissed him off hearing that his friend would even think about trying, there was no way he was going to let Eric take her to bed.

"You're mad, why?"

"Kiara is a sweet girl and I want you to stay away from her. If you're my friend you'll respect my wishes to leave her alone. There are plenty of other women on that site for you to choose from, pick one of them."

"Alright, but you better slow down pal, you're liking her way too much. I'll see you later and have fun at your sister's place when you go for dinner. I take it you aren't going to tell her about your little arrangement."

"No, no way is she to find out," he answered, showing Eric to the door. He then went to see what she was doing, he found her laying on the bed looking through a magazine. Going over he laid down next to her.

"Your friend seems nice," she said, putting the magazine down. "Does he know about me, what I'm doing here?"

"Yes, he knows." He saw how sad she looked and knew what she was thinking. "You have nothing to worry about, he won't tell anyone. We have a few hours before we have to be at my sister's place," he said, reaching over he started undoing the buttons on her shirt.

"Neil, I just got my period, I'm so sorry."

He stopped what he was doing to look at her, and couldn't help feeling a little disappointed. "It's alright, it can't be helped."

She could see by looking down that he was excited. "Just because you can't do anything to me doesn't mean I can't satisfy you." She straddled him, and opening his shirt she kissed down his chest, her fingers undoing his belt and pulling his zipper down. She moved down, taking him in her mouth she ran her tongue along his shaft, wrapping her mouth around him. With his pants down around his ankles, she gave him a blow job, making him grunt and moan when he came.

He had kicked his pants off when she started sucking, using her tongue to lick over the tip of his cock. Having him inside her mouth, feeling moist and warm drove him insane. His eyes rolled back, his heart drumming hard against his rib cage he let out a deep throaty moan when he came hard and fast. He pulled her up on top of him, waiting until he had his breathing under control.

She wiped her mouth, looking down at him while he had his eyes closed. Not having much experience doing that she was afraid at first that it wouldn't be any good for him. But hearing him moan and seeing the smile on his face she knew she did well. "I'll do better next time," she said, wanting to make him happy.

He opened his eyes in surprise. “Are you kidding me? I never had a BJ that good before. You did really well and thanks for doing that for me. I would like to know though just how long do your periods last?"

"They never last long, three, four days tops."

He rolled her over onto her back and got on top of her. "I will be counting the days," he said, lowering his head and kissing her. When he got up he pulled his pants on. "I'll have to stop at the store to buy some more condoms. We'll need them when your cycle is over," he said, looking at her he winked.

Later they changed their clothes and got ready to leave.

"What have you told your sister about me?"

He pulled her onto his lap, putting his arm around her waist. "Don't worry, I didn't tell her the truth. I told her we've been dating for a while and that you work for me, in the casino as a waitress. You have nothing to be worried about, they'll love you, just be your sweet self."

She did feel better, she hated the thought of people knowing what she really did. "I don't like lying to people, it doesn't seem right. On the other hand, I don't want them to know the truth about me or they will be disgusted."

He pulled her head down to kiss her, it was a soft, sweet kiss. "We better get going, Judy hates it when I'm late."

Chapter 3

He pulled into his sister's driveway and she looked at the house in front of her. "What a beautiful home," she said, admiring it when they stepped out of the car. "I can only dream of living in a place like this."

"Maybe you will someday," he said, taking her hand as they walked up to the front door and he rang the bell.

It opened and a woman who resembled Neil smiled at them. "You're on time for once," she said and stepped aside for them to enter. "You must be Kiara, I'm so happy to meet you. My brother was right, you really are beautiful. Come on in and meet my husband and daughter."

When they entered the living room a little girl with dark hair jumped up and ran into Neil's arms.

"Uncle Neil," she squealed when he started tickling her.

"How's my favorite little girl?"

"I'm really good Uncle Neil," she said, then looked at Kiara. "Is she your girlfriend?

Mommy said you were bringing her."

"Well, she's a girl and my friend so I guess you could say she's my girlfriend. Chrissy, meet my friend Kiara," he said to his niece when he put her down.

"Hi, you're pretty."

Kiara got down to her level. "Hi, I'm happy to meet you and I must say you are very pretty. I love your dress."

"Uncle Neil bought it for me for my birthday and a kitten. Would you like to see him?" she asked, beaming with joy.

"I would love to."

"I'll go get him," she answered back and took off in search of her kitten.

"Hi, I'm Roy, welcome to our home, please have a seat. I know what Neil likes to drink but what can I get you, dear?"

"A glass of wine would be nice thanks," she said, sitting down next to Neil. "You have a beautiful home," she said to Judy, taking the wine from Roy.

"Thank you.", I'll give you a tour later if you

"I'd love one, thanks."

Moments later Chrissy came bouncing into the room holding a tiny black and white kitten. “Here he is,” she said, going over and standing next to Kiara.

She set her wine down to pet the kitten. "Oh he's so sweet, can I hold him?"

The little girl smiled, handing him over to her.

"He's adorable, what's his name?"

"Mittens," Chrissy answered, hopping from one foot to the other. "I named him that because it looks like he is wearing mittens on his feet."

"OK sweetheart, take mittens to your room."

"OK mom, can I play in my room?"

"Yes, we'll call you when it's time for dinner."

Chrissy turned to Kiara and took the kitten from her. "Are you staying for dinner too, with Uncle Neil?"

"Yes, I'm staying," she said, smiling at her.

"Kiara, you have just made a friend of my daughter. Most people won't even look at her kitten much less touch it. Do you like animals?" Judy asked, taking a sip of her wine.

"Yes, I love all animals. I find them to be loving and won't hurt you as some people do. Chrissy is very sweet and cute as a button." She looked up to see them all watching her and wondered if she had said something wrong.

"So how did you and my big brother meet?"

She looked at him and remembered what he told her their story was going to be. "I came to work for him in the casino as a waitress. I hadn't been there very long when he first asked me out. At first, I thought it wasn't a good idea since he was my boss but he was so charming he wore me down so I agreed to go out with him." She looked back at him and smiled before going on. "I'm really glad I met him, he's so kind and treats me well."

Neil sat back, watching and listening to her lie. He thought she was way too good at it and thought maybe Eric was right. Maybe she was acting around him, telling him lies, ones to make him think she was sweet and innocent. He might not be her first client after all, could she be wanting to get her claws into him? She wouldn't be the first woman to lie to try and get him to put a ring on their finger.

His suspicions were growing, filling his head with doubt about her.

"So where did you work before?" Judy asked.

"What is this Judy? Let her relax without a ton of questions being thrown at her and you wonder why I never bring my dates over."

"You're right Neil," she said, then turned to Kiara. "I apologize, no more questions, let's just enjoy the evening."

After talking for a while Judy said she was going to check on dinner and Kiara offered to help and followed her into the kitchen. There she helped with the finishing touches and helped set the table.

When the women left the room it gave the guys a chance to talk.

"Kiara is a lovely young woman, mind if I ask how old she is?" Roy asked, pouring them another drink.

"She's twenty-two."

"Twenty-two, are you sure about that?" he asked, he raised his eyebrows.

"Yeah, why?"

"I'm a good judge of character and of people's ages. She seems younger to me, like maybe nineteen. Never mind me, there are some people who look much younger than their age, she must be one of the lucky ones."

"Kiara is one of the sweetest women I've ever met but sometimes I feel like she is hiding something from me."

"Like what?" Roy asked, sitting back down in his seat.

"I don't know, it's like she's afraid of something, or someone. But then we only recently just got together so maybe she's just still a little nervous around me."

"I could do some checking for you if you want me to."

Neil leaned over and stared at Roy. "Promise me you won't do that. She has a right to her privacy and if she ever found out she would never forgive me. I don't want to risk having her leave before our time is up."

Roy frowns. "What does that mean, before your time is up?"

Shit, he knew he had said too much so he tried to brush it off. "You know me, I don't stay with one woman for too long. I'm not done with her yet so I'd like to keep seeing her until the novelty wears off, you know what I'm talking about."

"Oh I see, you're still a dog. Alright, I'll stay out of her business and yours. I do hope you don't break her heart though."

Nothing else was said about the subject when Judy came in to let them know dinner was on the table. Chrissy insisted on sitting next to Kiara who paid attention to the little girl, talking to her and listening to her.

"You're really good with children," Judy said, smiling at Chrissy and pleased at how well-behaved she was being.

"It's easy with her, she's so adorable."

"Would you like to have children someday?"

"Judy please, you said you'd stop with the questions," Neil said with some anger in his tone, giving her a look that said he was not happy with her.

"I'm sorry, it was just a simple question."

She didn't want Neil to fight with his sister, especially with Chrissy right there. "It's alright. I love children and I hope someday to have a couple of my own, but that won't be for a very long time."

After the meal and cleaning up Judy took the little girl up for her bath before bedtime, Kiara stayed with the men. Chrissy came flying into the living room in her pajamas and jumped onto her lap.

"Would you tuck me into bed and read me a bedtime story, please?" she asked, holding her hands together prayer-like.

She looked over at Judy when she spoke. “I'd love to if it's alright with your mother."

Judy smiled and nodded. “It's alright with me, but give your daddy and uncle a kiss goodnight first."

After kissing them she took Kiara's hand and started dragging her along. Having been given a tour of the house earlier she knew where Chrissy's room was.

Judy turned to Neil when they were gone. "I like her, she's so nice and Chrissy seems to have taken quite a liking to her. I hope you don't end up hurting this one. Are you serious about her or are you just using her for sex?"

"Now sister, you know better than to ask me about my personal life. Kiara and I are having fun, it's nothing serious, we both know the score."

"She's not like the others, even you must see that." She could tell by looking at him that he had feelings for her, even if he wouldn't admit it to himself.

He didn't want to fight with her so he got to his feet. "I'm just going to go upstairs and see how they're doing," he said and walked out of the room. When he got to Chrissy's room he leaned against the door frame and watched them.

Kiara sat next to her on the bed, reading Cinderella. When the story was over she laid the book down, unaware that he was there. "It's time for you to go to sleep now."

"Can I ask you something?" she asked.

"Anything," Kiara answered.

"My friend says that a cat is a stupid pet to have, she said when it gets bigger he won't like me and will scratch me. Will Mittens stop loving me?"

Seeing the tears in the little girl's eyes her heart melted. "Mittens are not a stupid pet. Cats are very loving and affectionate. It is true that when they get older they will sometimes act like they don't care and will ignore you but that doesn't mean he doesn't still love you. When they want some attention they'll come to you. As long as you love him, treat him well, he'll always love you." shot has been saved to/Pictures/Screenshot

"Really?"

"I promise sweetheart, now you really have to go to sleep," she said, giving her a kiss on the forehead. "Sweet dreams," she said, turning off the lamp that was next to the bed. She waited until Chrissy's eyes closed before turning to leave and was startled when she saw Neil standing there. She walked over to where he was.

"You're really good with her," he said in a whisper, trapping her between his arms, her back against the door frame. He then lowered his head and kissed her softly on the lips, he stopped when he heard Chrissy giggle.

"Uncle Neil, I saw you kissing Kiara."

He went over and kissed her cheek. "You little monkey, you're supposed to be sleeping, now close your eyes before I tell your mom." He chuckled when she quickly shut her eyes. Walking away they went back downstairs.

They were each handed another drink and sat down to talk some more.

"So if you get lonely when Neil goes to Italy for a couple of weeks you can always come over here to hang out," Judy said, and then she noticed the look on both of their faces. "What?" she asked him.

He takes Kiara's hand and holds it. "She won't be lonely, she's coming to Italy with me."

"Oh, is she now?"

"Is there a problem with that Judy?"

Her face turned a little red. "No, it's just that since Kiara just started working for you and is dating you, won't some of your other employees become jealous? What if they become resentful and turn against her?"

"If anyone has a problem they know where the door is, I won't let anyone disrespect Kiara."

"But isn't it too soon for you both to be going on a vacation together to the most romantic place on earth?"

Roy was listening and figured it was time to step in before the brother and sister got into an argument. "Now Judy, they are both consenting adults and old enough to make their own decisions. Let them go and have some fun."

"Roy thanks, but I really think we should go home now," Neil said and stood, pulling Kiara up with him.

"Wait, don't go yet, it's still early and I made your favorite dessert, apple crumble pie with homemade ice cream. Roy's right and I'm sorry, you both deserve to have a good time. Will you stay awhile longer?" she asked, looking at her brother.

"Well, you know how much I love your apple pie so yeah, we'll stay."

So they stayed and had coffee and pie. The evening ended on a happy note, with promises of coming back again. He drove them home, stopping first at the store he ran in and came back out with a small bag, smiling as he pulled out the box of condoms.

"I'm counting the days until I can make love to you, so I want to be prepared."

She shook her head but smiled, she too was counting the days. Well, what could she say? He was so amazing in bed and she was already craving him.

They were getting ready for bed when Neil answered a call, hearing who it was he looked over at Kiara and frowned. "Yes, I'm very pleased with her. Yes, she has done everything I asked without questioning it. Listen, I don't want to be rude but don't call me again. My time is not up with her and I plan on enjoying every minute of it with her now goodnight," he said and hung up.

She sat up in bed listening to his end of the conversation. She wanted to ask him what they said but was too afraid.

When he looked at her he saw the fear creep back up in her eyes, he went and sat next to her. "I wish you would tell me why you're scared of them. I don't understand, you work for them so what's going on?"

"Nothing," she said, shaking her head.

He lifted her chin up with his fingers. "By the time we come back from Italy, you will have told me what's going on." He kissed her before getting undressed and climbing into bed.

"Do you want me to satisfy you?" she asked, knowing they couldn't have sex even though he wanted to.

He laid on his back. "Not tonight, but thanks for offering."

She lay on her side, she placed her hand on his chest as he slept. The feel of his beating heart under her hand felt so nice. It hit her that she had to stop acting scared so that he would stop asking questions, and pressuring her to tell him the truth about herself. From now on she would shower him with affection, making sure she pleased him so that way he would forget about knowing more about her.

For two days he was kept busy with work, making sure people were assigned to take care of his business during his absence. For this, she was grateful as she still had her period and hoped it would stop soon. Her wish came true, in four days it was gone and they would be heading to Italy the next morning.

She woke up and heard the shower running, knowing he was in there she decided to join him, something she would never have done before. His back was to her when she quietly stepped in, putting her arms around him, moving them down to his cock, her lips pressed against his back she started kissing it, hearing him moan and his cock growing hard in her hand.

The moment he felt her behind him he started getting hard, and when she put her hands on his shaft it grew harder and it started to throb. He had been without sex for almost four days and he was more than ready to be inside her hot pussy. He turned around, pushing her up against the wall, taking her hands, and placing them over the nozzle. "Keep them here," he growled, his breathing becoming ragged.

His hand moved down and between her legs, feeling how wet she was as he sucked hard on her neck, her moans only got him more excited. Feeling her breasts on his chest as they heaved hard against him he wanted to be inside her so badly but he didn't have a condom with him. "I want to fuck you so bad but I don't have anything with me," he said, his hard cock pressing against her.

"But I do," she said through breathy pants, opening her eyes to look at him.

Seeing the condom in her hand he smiled and took it from her, opening it and placing it over his manhood. Lifting her one leg up he entered her with one hard thrust, enjoying her moans. Lifting her other leg up and holding her under her ass he started pumping inside her, her back slamming against the wall. It felt so good being inside her warmth as she clamped her muscles around his cock. He came so hard and fast, making her gasp and scream out his name. He buried his face in her neck waiting for his breathing to go back to normal.

She kept her arms around his neck, her legs around his waist, tears fell down her face and she was glad that the running water was disguising them. The fullness of him filled her to the core, he had once again hit her g-spot, causing her to have the most amazing orgasm ever.

"Do you have any idea how fucking hot you are?" he asked, his lips caressing her neck before moving up to her lips.

"Oh, Neil." It was all she was able to get out before he kissed her passionately, his tongue slipping inside her mouth and his cock still hard he began thrusting inside her again, this time it was rough, hard as he pounded inside her, satisfying his lust.

Because of the thickness and length of him, it felt like her insides were going to burst apart, but it did feel amazing and she came fast, her juices running down his legs mixed with the water falling over them from the faucet. She didn't realize her nails were digging into his flesh until later when she saw the marks she left.

"Sweet mother of God you are something else baby, only you have ever succeeded in making me lose control like this," he said when he pulled out of her and put her down on her feet. He wrapped his arms around her, holding her so close he was almost afraid he was crushing her bones but since she didn't complain he kept his hold on her. It felt so good, their bodies pressed against each other as the water flowed over them.

She looked up at him and smiled as she ran her fingers over his lips. "You bring out what has been buried inside me my whole life, the desire, the lust. My entire body comes alive with just one touch from you. All those women you have made love to were so lucky to have even one night with you."

He stared deep into her eyes, his cock pressing against her. "I'll let you in on a secret, I have never put this much energy or time into making love to them that I have with you. You're different, special and so damn loving and affectionate. You make me want to give you my all, you make me feel like a real man," he said, lifting her head up and kissing her with so much passion.

She put her arms around him, hanging on as his mouth devoured hers. Her eyes closed she felt his cock getting hard again and knew he was going to take her again.

He released her, turning off the water he picked her up and carried her back to the bedroom, and laid her down, both still wet. Grabbing a condom from the nightstand he put it on and entered her, she was wet in more ways than one.

She lay curled up in his arms, her insides sore from all the sex they were having in such a short time. "Wow, you sure made up for our lost time," she said, snickering.

"You haven't seen anything yet, just wait until we get to Italy."

The next morning their bags were packed and they headed to the airport. She had never flown before and was excited, even more so when she found out they were flying first class. He let her have the window seat and when the plane took off they were each handed a glass of champagne. It annoyed her that the flight attendant was flirting with him but she kept her feelings hidden from him. It seemed no matter where they went, women were coming on to him and it was like he never even noticed it.

When they finally landed in Italy he had a rental car waiting for them and he drove them straight to the hotel. She felt like a kid at Christmas as she bounced from room to room in the suite he had booked.

"This place is amazing, so beautiful. Everywhere I've ever lived was never this big and look at the view," she said, running out onto the balcony.

He smiled and going up behind her he put his arms around her waist and rested his head against hers. "Where have you lived my kitten?" He was hoping that she would tell him, tell him anything at all about herself.

There were a few moments of silence between them before she spoke.

"Let's go for a walk," she said, changing the subject.

"Ok, it's a nice night out and I'll take you to this really nice outdoor cafe where we can get something to eat."

They walked along a path that led to some small shops and a mini-market. Most of the buildings had apartments above the shops and music drifted out through the open windows. Everyone was in a good mood, talking and laughing and waving to them as they passed by. Neil, knowing the language would greet them with a hello or it's a lovely evening.

She was impressed and told him so. “You speak the language perfectly, almost as if you were born here."

"My mother was Italian, she taught me."

"Your father, he wasn't Italian. I'll take it."

"No, American."

"Are they both deceased?"

He smiled at her. "For someone who won't tell me anything about herself you sure do ask me a lot of questions about myself."

"I'm sorry, I shouldn't have asked, it's none of my business."

"It's alright, I have nothing to hide. Judy and I were born late in their lives. Dad was almost sixty when I was conceived, and my mom was in her fifties. He had a heart attack about four years ago, he had a long and good life. My mother passed away a year later, she never got over his death."

She put her arm through his as they kept walking. "I'm so sorry, they must have been deeply in love."

"They were right up to the day they passed away. They met and started dating in high school and were happily married. Not many couples can say that nowadays. Dad took me into the business as soon as I was done with college, and he taught me everything I know today. I loved working with him side by side. It's just not the same without him."

"I bet if they were alive today they would be so proud of you," she said, looking up at him. "What about Judy, did she not want to be part of the business?"

"No, she never cared about it, she preferred to be a wife and stay-at-home mother. She does get a percentage of the profits and has some shares in the business." He stopped when they were in front of a quaint little outdoor cafe. "Let's eat here, the food is fantastic."

They were seated when a waiter came out to take their order. He ordered both of them, knowing she would like the pasta and veal along with a bottle of wine.

He sat back watching her as she ate, still wanting to know more about her. "Do you believe in love?" he asked, pouring her another glass of wine.

"No," she answered without looking up from her plate.

This surprised him, she was way too young not to believe in love. "Why not?"

"No reason really, I just don't."

"Weren't your parents in love? he asked, hoping that by slipping it in she might trip up and tell him something, and he was right.

"Hell if I know, my father left after I was born."

"I'm sorry to hear that."

She narrowed her eyes when she looked back at him. "You're very sneaky Neil, you tricked me into telling you something about me."

"What about your mother?"

If you must know my mother and I were never close. She was a drug addict and was more interested in getting high and sleeping around. She died of an overdose a year ago. Before you ask, I don't have any siblings or other relatives."

He reached over and placed his hand over the top of hers. "I'm so sorry, it sounds like you've had a hard life. But why did you decide to go into this business?"

"Why do you think so? It was for the money. I worked as a waitress when I could find the work but I never had enough to make ends meet. When I heard about this job I thought it sounded great, all I had to do was go on dates." She knew she had said too much, and knew he would have more questions but she had to keep quiet.

"Are you telling me you didn't know that sleeping with the clients was part of the job?" When she didn't answer he kept pushing. "If that's the case you don't have to, just tell them you can't do the job."

She dropped her fork onto the plate and pushed it away from her. "I don't want to talk about it anymore. I've already broken the rules by telling you my real name and now this. Please, will you stop asking me questions?"

"I'll stop for now." Seeing she was done eating and talking he paid for their meal and they walked back to the hotel.

Chapter 4

When they get back to the hotel he takes her hand and walks to the bedroom, he removes his shirt and pulls her into his arms. It was the sweetest feeling when she put her arms around his neck and kissed him back. He lowered her down onto the bed, his hands on each side of her his kiss turned more passionate. He heard her moaning and felt her fingers running through his hair.

"Oh yes," she purred when his hand went under her dress and his fingers slid inside her wet pussy. It always amazed her how quickly he could remove her clothes as she lay there naked and waited for him to remove his pants. She arched her back when he took one of her breasts in his mouth, it tickled when he flicked his tongue over her erect nipple. Her legs opened on their own accord when he got between them and entered her. She was so close to coming when he stopped and pulled out, flipping her onto her stomach. Putting his hands on her waist he lifted her up and slowly entered her. Biting down on the pillow she screamed when he started pounding into her, making her come fast then she felt his own release coming.

Her legs gave out and she laid flat on her stomach, his weight on top of her. She felt his cock sliding out and his hot breath on the back of her neck as he kissed her neck.

"That was amazing, we really have to start trying different positions," he said as he rolled off her and onto his side. He moved his hand up and down her back, his eyes on her face. "Was that the first time you had sex this way?"

"Yes," she said shyly.

"Oh shit, I'm sorry. If I had known I would have taken things a little slower. Did I hurt you?" he asked, feeling guilty.

"A little at first but then it felt good."

"Seeing that you are inexperienced I will take it easy when I introduce you to other ways of making love."

She looked at him shocked, she thought he was enjoying what they were already doing. "Am I not satisfying you now?"

He pulled her towards him, their bodies touching as he ran his hand down her back and up again. "Yes, you are, very much so.

It's just that there are so many different positions and ways of having sex. Like you being on top for one and my favorite is the blindfold and tying your hands to the bed."

"You like that kind of thing?" she asked, blushing.

"It gets me hard just thinking about you tied up and helpless while I explore every inch of you and watch you squirm. Are you up to any of that?"

"There won't be any hitting or whips will there?"

"No, I would never do anything to hurt you. I just want to spice things up in the bedroom, to give both of us pleasure. Also, I'm not into spanking women, but I would like to take you to places like a public washroom or up against the wall in an alleyway."

"What if we were to get caught?" she said, smiling when she looked at him.

"I'll make sure we won't." Giving her another kiss he laid on his back and went to sleep. Waking up through the night he found her laying with her head on his chest, her hand over his stomach. Now he wasn't one to cuddle, even after sex but he didn't have the heart to move her. So he put his arm around her and went back to sleep.

Waking up to find his arm around her she smiled, he had told her he never cuddled and here he was. Feeling frisky she moved her hand down to his cock, taking a hold of it as she started kissing his chest. Soon she felt him growing hard and heard him moaning and his fingers going through her hair. Remembering what he had said about trying positions she decided to try it, so she climbed on top and straddled him.

His lips curled up into a smile, his hands going on her hips. "What do we have here?"

"I'm going to ride you," she said, opening the condom package. Once she placed it over his shaft she put him near her pussy which was already wet, then she lowered herself slowly down until she had all of him inside her. "Oh God," she groans, her head going back as she starts moving up and down on him. She liked how it felt when he started caressing both of her breasts and she started moving faster, feeling his cock pulsating inside her.

He knew they were both so close to coming so he put his hands on her ass as she continued to ride him hard. It was like an explosion ripping through him when he came, sparks of light lit up behind his closed eyes and he let out a loud grunt. She too let out a cry of pleasure, her head landing on his chest. He stroked the back of her head. "Wow, that was out of this world."

Getting off him she laid on her side, watching as he got up and went to the bathroom. He came back after getting rid of the condom and got back in next to her. "Did I take it well?" she asked, running her fingers over his chest.

"Oh my God, you were amazing," he said, pulling her into his arms. "Let's shower and then go get something to eat."

After they ate he took her to the Uffizi Gallery where there were many paintings from some famous artists, such as Leanardo da Vinci, Raphael, and many others. He got a kick out of how her eyes lit up as she went from one painting to another.

"I never thought for one minute that I would ever get to see these paintings. I've seen them in magazines, not in real life. They are so much more beautiful in person and this gallery is spectacular. Thanks for bringing me here."

"I'm glad you like it and I have much more to show you while we're here."

She stopped and stood in front of him. "You got me as your sex kitten, you don't have to do all this for me. You could go places yourself and leave me at the hotel until you're ready for sex. You might even find another woman to show you around."

Taking her arm he led her around the corner, away from prying eyes. Putting her up against the wall, his hands resting on the wall by her head. "Let's get one thing straight. If I wanted to meet a woman here I wouldn't have brought you with me. Not only do I want to enjoy you sexually I also want you to go places with me, to be my companion." He lowered his head to kiss her, it was turning passionate until they heard someone shout out.

"Break it up, go somewhere else if you want to do that."

Neil turned his head to see one of the gallery guards glaring at them. Taking her hand they walked past the guard and left the building.

"There's a bar up ahead, we'll go there and have a couple of drinks and a bite to eat."

They ordered a pitcher of beer and some wings, then another pitcher of beer. It was getting late by the time he ordered the third pitcher. He knew she was getting drunk but since she was having fun he let her carry on. She even dragged him onto the dance floor and started grinding up against him.

"You're making me horny," he said when she placed her hand over his crotch.

"Me too," she said, putting her arms around his neck. "We could go outside, around the back, and make out."

He laughed, pulling her closer to her. “I think you're drunk."

"I am a little drunk. But wasn't it you that said you wanted to have sex with me in an alleyway or a public washroom?"

His tongue swept over his bottom lip when he looked down at her. "You really want to do this?" he asked, hoping she'd say yes. When she smiled back at him he knew he had his answer. Taking her hand he went to the bar and paid the bill, they then walked outside.

Once outside he led her around the building, it was dark in the alley except for the one dim light that hung over the back door. He wasted no time in pinning her up against the wall with her hands above her head with one hand, his other hand went under her dress and inside her panties. He stroked inside her, making her wetter than she was. His mouth sucked on her neck, making her moan.

Their adrenaline was pumping, their breathing stuttering with every breath they took. He released her and pulled down her panties, taking them off her. Pulling down his zipper he lifted her up, ordering her in a demanding tone, and told her to wrap her legs around him. His mouth came down hard on hers when he entered her with one hard thrust.

She was a quivering mass of pleasure as he pounded his cock into her, making her back slam into the wall. He moved fast, and hard, making her gasp with each thrust of his cock. With two more hard thrusts, they both came, and she clung to him for dear life. She felt weak, her insides on fire from his brute force and attack on her throbbing pussy.

Pulling out he set her down on her feet but held on when he felt her legs buckle. “That was mind-blowing," he said, and cupping her face in his hand he smiled at her. "You're so fucking beautiful when you come."

"You liked it?" she asked, wanting to please him.

"He let her go and did up his zipper. “Oh yeah, I liked it very much. I can't believe you suggested this but boy am I ever glad you did."

"Well, that's what I'm here for, to give you what you want."

"Excuse me," he snapped. "So you did this just because you thought it was what I wanted?"

"It is what you wanted wasn't it?"

He picked up her panties and threw them at her. "Put these on." He was angry, angry at her for only doing it for him and not because she also wanted it.

She was confused by his change of attitude, of how angry he had become. She slipped her panties back on, stumbling in the process. . She tried to catch up to him as he started walking back to their hotel. "Neil, wait up, you're walking too fast, I can't keep up."

He stopped and waited for her to catch up, his jaw twitched. He was hoping he would cool down by the time they reached the hotel.

"What's wrong, why are you mad?" she asked when she caught up to him.

"Don't talk to me right now," he said starkly.

She felt hurt, not knowing what had changed between them, it didn't help that she was half in the bag and having trouble walking. "Neil, I'm having trouble walking, can I hold onto your arm?"

He stopped to look at her before putting his arm around her waist. They walked the rest of the way without speaking to each other. Once he got her inside their suite he let go of her and walked over to the liquor cabinet and poured himself another drink.

She stood there looking at him. "Aren't you coming to bed?"

"No, you go ahead, I'll be in shortly."

Her lips quivered, wondering what she had done wrong. But not wanting to anger him any further she went into the bedroom. She stripped out of her clothes and the room started to spin so laying down she passed out.

Neil sat stewing in his anger, many thoughts went through his head. Was she more of a pro than he thought she was, Were her sweet innocent ways just an act? He finished his drink and headed to the bedroom. There he found her butt naked on the bed, laying on her stomach. God, he had to admit she had a great ass and found himself getting hard. Shaking it off he covered her with the blankets and removing his clothes he went and took a cold shower.

He came out after drying off and got into bed, turning to look at her. She looked like a sweet, innocent angel as she slept. He hated the thought that she was playing him for a sucker and tomorrow he would tell her what he thought of her and knew what she was playing at. But for now, he needed sleep so turning his back to her he closed his eyes and went to sleep.

She woke up feeling like crap, her head felt like it was going to explode and her throat was so dry it hurt. Getting out of bed she put on what was closest to her, his shirt. She looked at him sleeping before going into the tiny kitchen and pouring herself a large glass of water. She then started the coffee, knowing that Neil would want one when he woke up. It still bothered her the way he turned from a loving into an angry man. She looked up when she saw him enter the kitchen and poured them both some coffee, handing one to him. Her heart began to race when she saw him shirtless, his defined muscles still damp from the shower he must have taken while she was in making the coffee.

He didn't look at her when he took the mug from her and sat down. But when she went up behind him, putting her arms around his neck, and started kissing his neck he pushed her away. "You can knock off the act, kitten," he said, emphasizing the word kitten.

Shocked, she pulled away. "What?" she asked, walking around to face him."

"You heard me," he snapped.

"I don't understand, what act?"

He banged his fist on the table, making her jump. "Pretending that you like what we've been doing. Do they teach you how to fake your orgasms and how to act like you are enjoying being with the client? Are you taking me for some kind of fool?" take

Tears sprang to her eyes. "What's gotten into you and why are you talking to me like this?"

"When I was fucking you in that alleyway you made a comment."

"What comment?" she asked, trying to hold back her tears.

"You said that's why you're here, to give me what I want."

"Well it's true, that's why you called the site and picked me."

"So you were faking all along, you just fed my ego, and you let me think you were enjoying it as much as I was."

"Neil, we are told to give the clients whatever they want, to do whatever they say. We were told to fake it, to pretend but I wasn't pretending with you. I came to you planning on doing so but I liked being with you. I never once faked my orgasm and as for having to give you whatever you wanted, well, I wanted to please you and not because they told me I had to."

He watched as she walked over to the counter, though her back was to him he knew she was crying. Getting up he goes over and puts his hands on her shoulders. "I'm sorry. I should have discussed it with you before jumping to conclusions. You have to understand that even though I'm paying for your time I still want to know that you are being honest and also enjoying us being together."

"The way you talked to me, it made me feel cheap, like a whore."

He swung her around to face him. "Don't say that. You're not a whore."

She lowered her eyes. "But you're paying to have sex with me, so that does make me one, a prostitute."

He cupped her face in his hand and lifted her face up so that he could look into her eyes. "No, you're not. You don't belong in this business, I can see that and I want you to quit."

"I can't, they won't let me."

"What do you mean they won't let you?"

"Neil please, just drop it."

Seeing how upset she was and how pale his heart went out to her. "You will tell me before we leave here to go back home. But now I have a breakfast meeting to attend. I'll order you some room service and then you go back to bed and get some rest. You look like death warmed over."

"I do feel sick from all that beer I drank last night."

He pulled her into his arms, he felt like a heel for the way he treated her. "I'll be back as soon as I can. I just need to talk to someone about the new machines that I'm thinking of bringing into my casino."

After ordering her some room service he made her go to bed while he got dressed and when her food came he took it to her. Giving her a kiss he left for his meeting.

Not being able to eat much of the food she went back to sleep, waking two hours later. Neil still wasn't back so she went and took a quick shower and then after drying off she put his shirt back on. Feeling more like herself she goes to make some coffee and to have a drink of water, she vowed never to drink that much ever again.

She looked up from her coffee when she heard him walk in, in his hands were some flowers. She felt her heart racing when he walked over to her and touched the side of her face.

"You look much better than you did earlier. I'm sorry I took so long and especially about this morning. I got these flowers for you, hoping you'll forgive me."

Putting her coffee down she takes the flowers from him and smells them. "They're beautiful but you, I didn't have to get them for me. I had already forgiven you. Honestly, you did have every right to feel the way you did. I would have felt the same way if I were in your shoes."

Taking the flowers from her he placed his hands around her waist and lifted her up onto the counter. Getting between her legs he put one hand on her leg, the other one going around her waist, and pulled her close. He didn't speak, he just started kissing her. He slowly continued kissing her as his hand moved to the buttons on the shirt she was wearing, undoing them until her breasts were exposed.

She tilted her head back when he moved to her breast, putting one in his mouth, and started sucking, nibbling on the nipple. Feeling his hand move down between her legs she opened them wider, letting him finger her. Leaning back she moaned, her hips pushing against his fingers as he stroked her into a climax. She opened her eyes to look at him when he pulled out, and her eyes widened when he licked his fingers, smiling at her.

"You taste so sweet," he said, then pulled his top off over his head and threw it down before he picked her up and carried her to the bedroom.

Two hours later he rolled off her and looked at her as he lay on his side. "You're so beautiful," he said, putting his hand on her breasts. He loved the way they felt, so soft yet firm. "Has anyone ever told you what amazing breasts you have?"

"No," she said, looking into his eyes, his hand felt so warm on her skin.

"Well, you do. I was going to take you on a wine tour but I have a feeling after last night you won't feel like doing any wine tasting. So we'll go visit The Leaning Tower of Pisa, how does that sound to you?"

"I'd like that," she answered.

Taking a quick shower and changing they headed out and when they got there they climbed up to the viewing platform. She went from one end to the other, looking around at the view. "Oh Neil, the view from up here is spectacular, you can see everything."

He stood behind her, putting his arms around her waist. "Whenever I come to Italy I always come here. There's something peaceful about being here and looking out over the city. I knew you would love it."

She turned around to face him, putting her arms around his neck. "You were right. I never in my wildest dreams thought I'd be in Italy, thank you for bringing me with you." Pulling his head down she kissed him.

Neil was taken by surprise by her public display of affection but still, he liked it, maybe a little too much when he felt his cock getting hard. "We better stop now or I'll be looking for somewhere to do some unthinkable things to you. As much as I like the thrill of doing it in public places, this is a little too public."

She giggled when she felt his hardness pressing against her. "I'm hungry, I haven't eaten since this morning."

"What would you like?"

"I noticed a small pizza place when we were driving here and with the window down in the car I could smell it. It smelled delicious."

"Then we'll eat there," he said, giving her one more kiss before leaving to go have something to eat.

The pizza place was owned and run by an older couple who greeted them when they walked in and got them seated. Neil talked to him in Italian, they chatted for a few minutes before he ordered a large deluxe and two glasses of red wine.

The older man, who everyone was calling papa kept talking to him, every now and then he would look at her. She was curious as to what they were talking about, she would soon find out.

Neil could tell she was wondering what was going on, he leaned over the table. "Papa asked if we were Americans and if you were my wife. I told him no but that we are together and he wants to know if we would like to go in back and help make our pizza."

"You're kidding, do they really let their customers do that?"

"I guess, so do you want to?"

She smiled. "It might be fun, let's do it."

He had some more words with Papa and they followed him into the back where they were introduced to his wife and son, Marcel. Neil took one look at the son and wished he had declined the offer. The young man looked like a God, his skin was tanned, he had dark hair and he was looking at her like he wanted to devour her. Typical Italian, always flirting with women, he thought to himself.

Marcel showed them how to roll the dough and put it on the pan, then he told them to put on the sauce and any toppings they wanted. He did speak to her in broken English and laughing he went behind her and taking her hand helped her spread the sauce.

"This is the proper way to do it," he said, smiling at her. "You are very good, you like?" he asked her as Neil looked on.

Once the toppings were on Marcel placed them in the oven. Neil took her hand and turned to the young man. "Thank you but we'll be sitting down now," he said in Italian. What he wanted to do was punch the guy in the face but out of respect for Mama and Papa, he held back.

"That was so much fun," she said when they were seated and took a sip of her wine.

"Which part, making the pizza or having him stand behind you with his arms around you?" he said with a hint of anger in his voice. She looked hurt and knew which part she enjoyed, and it wasn't the guy. "Could you not tell that he was hitting on you?"

She looked down at her wine. "He was just being nice and it was making the pizza that I enjoyed." She looked up at him. "I would have preferred having you behind me but he was just showing me the right way to do things."

He reached over and took her hands in his. "I was jealous when I saw how close he got to you, I wanted to punch him."

"There's no reason to be jealous, I'm here with you."

"Marcel is one gorgeous man, are you saying you're not in the least bit attracted to him?"

"He is good looking but you are more handsome. I'm not stupid, I know he's a player and was flirting. I don't like men who come on to a woman when the man she is with is right there. It shows a lack of respect on his part."

Just then the pizza arrived and Papa asked if they enjoyed making their own meal. Getting an answer that had him beaming ear to ear left them to enjoy the pizza.

When they were done and he went to pay the bill Papa refused to take their money. All he asked was that they come back and tell their friends. As they were leaving Marcel came from out back and as he was walking towards her she moved closer to Neil, putting her arm around his waist, and felt his going over her shoulder. They both knew that the young man was going to hug her, or worse, kiss her.

Marcel stopped when he saw the way they grabbed onto each other. "I just wanted to wish you both a good evening and I hope to see you again," he said, looking right at her.

Once outside he pulled her into his arms. "Why did you put your arm around me?"

She smiled sweetly up at him. "I wanted to give him the message that I'm with you and am not interested in him."

"I like that," he said, lowering his head and giving her a long passionate kiss. "Let's go back to the hotel so that I can give you a great deal of pleasure."

Chapter 5

The next day he took her on a wine tour at one of the most famous wineries in Italy. First, they were shown around the grounds where the grapes were, then it was back to the building for the tasting of their different wines.

"Try this one," an older gentleman said, handing them both a glass of red wine. "You'll find it to have a smooth taste."

Neil recognized the man, he too was from Las Vegas and owned one of the other casinos. "Mr. Driver, what a surprise to find you here in Italy."

"My wife and I are here on vacation." He looks at her, takes her hand, and kisses the back of it. "Who is this lovely creature you're with?"

Neil introduced them. "So where is your wife?"

"The poor dear had a headache and wasn't up to coming. Why don't we make plans to have dinner tomorrow night?" After they exchanged phone numbers and the hotels where they were staying they made plans for the next night.

She never said anything to Neil but there was something in the way he looked at her that gave her the creeps. But since she was here and had to keep him happy she kept quiet about her feelings since he seemed to be friends with the man.

Having had more wine than she was used to she asked if they could go for a walk and get some fresh air.

Taking her hand they walked through the field, after twenty minutes he stopped and turned to her, and put his hands on her hips. "Are you feeling better now?"

"Yes. I think it was the wine and it was so hot in there that it got to me. But out here, though it's warm and sunny there is a nice breeze. I'll let you in on a secret, I also wanted to get you alone."

"Why?" he asked, wondering what she was up to.

"So I could do this." She pressed her body up against his, her lips going to his as she placed her arms around his neck. Maybe it was the wine or the fact that she was in a different country that made her feel free. Her kiss became urgent, more demanding as she forced her tongue inside his mouth, hearing him moan as his cock got hard, pressing against her.

He tightened his hold on her, his desire to have her was so strong he knew there was no waiting until they got back to the hotel. He tore his lips from hers and looked around. He spotted what looked like an old shack, one he knew they used to store tools and other items used to pick the grapes. "Come with me," he said, pulling her along.

"Where are we going?"

"Somewhere where I can fuck you." He looked at her and saw the look on her face. "Don't be so shocked, you started this when you kissed me the way you did. You got me so horny I want you now so it's either in that shack or right here in the field."

"But what if someone catches us?"

"This is Italy, people do it whenever and wherever they want to and people just go about their business, ignoring two lovers who are in the heat of passion. He opened the door and turned on the small lantern. It didn't give off much light but there was enough that he could see what they were doing. He locked the door and turning to her instructed her to take off her panties.

"Seriously, you want to do it here?"

"You can't get me all revved up and not expect me to walk away. Now take off your panties and come sit on my lap," he said, pulling down his pants and sitting down on the bench.

She gasped when she saw his manhood spring up and he placed his hand around it. But for the life of her, she found herself getting turned on and felt the pool of wetness between her legs. So, she slid down her panties slowly and walked over, and straddled him. She felt his warmth and hardness as he entered her when he guided her down on his cock.

"Ride me hard," he said into her neck when he started sucking, his one hand fondling her breasts over the material of her dress. He closed his eyes, it felt so good being inside her and if the ground wasn't so dirty he would have laid her down and fucked her. But to him, this was just as good, especially when he heard her scream when she orgasmed, then he too came.

She rested her head on his shoulder, she had to wonder what it would feel like to have raw sex with him, to feel him inside her without the condom.

He kissed the top of her head as he ran his hands down her back. "That was so hot but we better clean up and leave here before one of the workers comes." He lifted her head to kiss her. "You're the greatest, so affectionate and giving. I really like that you are willing to do what I want."

They walked hand in hand back up to the main building, her body was still warm from the sex and she hoped no one would notice how flushed she was. She often wondered if people could tell when someone just had sex. Was there some kind of sign that gave it away?"

Back at the main house, Neil was talking to the owner about his wine, he was thinking of having some sent to his hotel for his guests. When she caught Mr. Driver staring at her the hairs on the back of her neck stood up and she moved closer to Neil, draping her arm through his. She knew he didn't mind her clinging to him when he placed his hand over hers and smiled, it was like he liked her doing it.

When he was done talking to the owner and left he turned to her. "Are you alright?"

"Yes, why do you ask?"

"Oh I don't know, maybe it's the way you are hanging onto me like you're afraid. What has gotten you feeling this way?"

She glanced over at Steven Driver and seeing that he was still watching her she looked away. "It's nothing, I just had too much wine and am feeling a little tired."

He touched her chin with his hand. "It has been a long day for both of us. We can go back to the hotel now and order room service and stay in tonight."
He held on to her when they went to say goodbye to their host, then stopped to let Steven know what time they would be meeting him and his wife for dinner the next night.

She kept her eyes lowered as the two men talked, and Steven scared her. She was so happy when they finally left but was not happy about having to see him again. Her head started to ache, she knew a headache was coming so when they were back at the hotel she asked him if he had any aspirins.

Since he didn't, he went down to the lobby and bought a small bottle from the small shop that carried such things as magazines and other items.
She took the two pills he offered her along with a glass of water.

"You go lay down for a while and I'll order you some room service."

She put her arms around him, giving him a hug.
"OK, thank you for being so good to me and not getting angry."

"Why would I get angry with you?"

"I know you wanted to stay longer but left because of me."

"Hey, you were tired and I didn't mind leaving." He lifted her chin up. "There is only so much wine one can test in just a couple of hours. I found the wine I wanted for my hotel, that's all I wanted. Now, go get some rest and I'll wake you when our food arrives."

She was feeling much better when she woke up three hours later when the food arrived. Her stomach growled so loudly her face turned red when he looked at her and smiled. She covered her mouth and let out a giggle. "Excuse me," she said, smiling back at him.

Her smile warmed his heart, her beautiful green eyes sparkled when she did. "Someone's hungry," he said as they dug into their meal. He was glad to see she was feeling better, her face now had a rosy glow to it. That night he didn't attempt to make love to her, he thought he would let her rest. But if she were to make a move he wouldn't deny her what she wanted.

Getting out of bed in the morning she wondered where Neil was, he wasn't anywhere in the suite, but the coffee was already made so she poured herself a cup. Pouring a second cup she heard him come in so she got up and went into the other room. She saw a bag in his hands and was curious as to why he would go shopping so early in the morning.

"Morning sleepy head. I thought today we could relax by the pool before we go out to dinner tonight."

"I don't have a bathing suit."

"You do now," he said, opening the bag and pulling out two swimsuits for her and one for himself. "I hope you like the ones I picked out for you."

She takes them and checks them out, raising an eyebrow. "They're kind of skimpy."

"You have a great body, you should show it off." Taking the one from her he held it up. "Wear this one for me, it's my favorite," he said with a smirk on his face.

"I'll wear it for you but I will also be wearing a cover-up over it."

"We'll see," he answered back. "It's almost lunch, I'll order some food then later we'll go for a swim."

"Alright, I'll go take a shower."

His eyes lit up and he tore off his shirt. "I'll join you," he said and started chasing her into the bathroom, her laughter filling the room when she started running. He caught her, turned her around, and ripped the shirt she was wearing off her, the buttons falling to the floor. Moments later they were both in the shower, going at it like a couple of animals in heat.

Later when they were done eating they changed into their bathing suits and went down to the pool. Picking out a couple of chairs they laid down, he looks over at her, smiling.

"You can take off the shirt now, get some sun."

She looked around nervously, hoping no one was looking as she removed the shirt. "I'm not used to wearing a bikini, especially one so revealing."

"Well you look hot, just relax and look around. All the women are wearing the same so you're not alone," he said and he put on his sunglasses, laying back down. He turned to look at her as she lay there, her eyes closed. Then seeing how all the guys who walked past them checked her out he regretted buying her a suit that showed too much of her body off. Later he would throw it away, the other one was not as revealing.

He had closed his eyes and not ten minutes later he felt a drop of water hit his chest. He opened his eyes and saw a brunette standing over him, dripping wet holding a tube of lotion. Her very large breasts were practically popping out of her bikini top.

"Would you do a lady a favor and rub some of this on my back and chest?" she asked, smiling down at him.

He glanced over at Kiara whose lips were pressed tightly together and she turned her head, not looking at him. He jumps to his feet and faces the woman. "Sorry, no can do, my lady and I are going for a swim." Going over to her he pulls her up. "Time for a swim kitten."

In the water, as she was standing in front of him she smiled. "You could have done it, you know, rub the lotion on her."

He put his arms around her, pulling her closer. "The only chest I want to rub is yours." He then gave her a kiss, pressing his body against her.

They enjoyed the pool for over an hour before getting out to dry off. By this time the pool area was getting crowded and more men were eyeing her up and down. This was his cue for them to leave.

"We should go back to our room and shower, it'll soon be time to meet Steven and his wife for dinner."

Just hearing that man's name gave her a bad feeling, but she shrugged it off when Neil covered her up with the shirt she was wearing earlier. "I'm glad we came down for a swim, it was so refreshing. At first, I thought the water was going to be cold."

"It's a heated pool, are you ready to go up?" When she nodded he held her hand as they walked past the crowd, letting all the men there know she was with him.

That night she wore a white skirt and a pink top, her hands shook when she applied her lipstick, a pale pink one. She really had no idea why she was nervous about seeing Steven again. It's not like he did anything wrong, except for staring at her. She decided to let it go, maybe tonight she would feel different. After all, his wife would be there too. Her head turned to look at Neil when he walked into the bedroom, her stomach had butterflies in it just by looking at him. There was something about a man wearing a dark suit that made them look sexy.

He couldn't take his eyes off of her, no matter what she wore she looked beautiful. With her long slender legs, her tiny waist, and her firm, perky breasts she could be a model. He still couldn't believe his luck in finding her and having her all to himself for a month. "You look so beautiful. I know I say that a lot but it's true."

She blushed, walking up to him and straightening his tie. "Neil, thank you but you don't have to keep saying it. Also, I have to say you look so handsome in a suit, or even just in jeans and a shirt. I see how all the women look at you when you enter a room, they're practically drooling over you."

"Is that jealousy I hear in your voice?"

She looked at him and then quickly looked away. "I have no claim on you so I've no reason to be jealous."

There was an awkward pause before he spoke. "I guess we should go to dinner now." No matter what she said he could hear in her voice that she was jealous. He wasn't sure whether to be happy or sad about it.

Steven stood when Neil and Kiara walked over to the table, he shook his hand and leaned over and kissed her on the cheek, his hand lingering on her arm. "Neil, you know my wife," he said, then looked at her. Kiara, this is my wife Pauline."

They all sat down and the waiter brought over a bottle of wine, pouring them each a glass before taking their order. The men discussed their business while the women talked about everyday stuff.

"Neil, so tell us how you two met?" Pauline asked.

Talk about being put on the spot so he figured he would use the same story as he told his sister. "We met when she came to work for me as a waitress in my hotel, we started dating and here we are."

Steven's eyes narrowed. "I've never seen you there," he said, eyeing her.

"Now Steven, you don't pop in that often, and perhaps when you did it could have been her day off."

"You're right," he answered, nodding.

The meal came along with another bottle of wine and after eating they declined dessert. When Pauline pulled out some pictures of her trip to Spain and was showing Neil, Kiara excused herself to use the lady's room. So far the only bad vibe she got from Steven was when they first got there and his hand lingered on her arm, but since then he barely looked at her.

She came out of the washroom to find Steven standing there. She backed up when he came towards her, she wasn't sure what he was going to do but after looking into his eyes she felt fear creeping up through her.

He got close, way too close, and smiled at her. "I find myself drawn to you," he said as his eyes went to her chest. "Neil is such a lucky man to have you. I bet you're a hell of a firecracker in the sack."

Not wanting to be alone with him she pushed past him. "I have to get back to Neil."

"Don't rush off, kitten."

She stopped and turned to face him. "What did you say?"

He moved up to her and putting his hands on her arms shoved her up against the wall. "I know all about you, that you're from the Sex Kitten Site. What do you think will happen when Neil's family and business associates find out he hired a slut to have sex with him, it could ruin his reputation."

"What do you want?"

He looked down at her chest. "I think you know what I want. What I want is a few hours alone with you. So this is what you're going to do. You're going to slip him a sleeping pill and when he falls asleep you'll come to the room I've already booked, it's just around the corner from where you're staying now." He took out a white pill and shoved it in the tiny pocket on her skirt. When I'm done with you then you can go back to him. If you prove to be as good as I think you are, I'll call the site and book you for a few nights."

You're disgusting," she spat at him.

"Room 106, be there around ten."

"What about your wife?"

"I'll make sure she's fast asleep before then. I'm warning you, don't tell Neil or I'll destroy him," he said, then he shoved some money down her top and inside her bra. "This is just part of your tip for services rendered." He then walked away, going back into the dining room.

She leaned up against the wall, fighting to hold back her tears. She felt like she was going to throw up when his hand went down her top and she felt his fingers touching her breasts. She needed to calm her nerves before going back to the table. She wasn't sure how she was going to stand to be at the table with Steven there. Knowing she was taking too long she went back and sat down, moving closer to Neil.

"You were gone a long time," he said when she sat down.

"I'm sorry, I was feeling a little queasy, alright now." I'm

"It's getting late, we should go back to our room then you can get some rest." He turned to the others and pulled out his wallet. "It was a lovely evening, maybe we can get together again before our vacation ends."

"Put your wallet away Neil, it's our treat," Steven said, smiling over at Kiara.

When they got inside their room he was worried about her, she was so quiet and she wouldn't look at him. He cupped her face in his hands and made her look at him. "I know something is bothering you, tell me what it is."

"It's nothing," she said, removing his hands from her face as she walked away.

He followed her into the bedroom and watched as she started unbuttoning her blouse. "Did something happen at the restaurant?"

She turned to him, her eyes went wide with fear. "What?"

"Ever since you came back from the lady's room you were quiet, and you were gone way too long." He then noticed something poking out the top of her bra. He walked over to her and reaching into her bra pulled out two one hundred American dollar bills. "What the hell is this and where did you get it?"

She had forgotten about the money and was shocked when he reached in and took the money. He looked so angry that for the first time since she had been with him was scared, biting down on her bottom lips she couldn't look at him.

"TELL ME," he screamed at her, making her jump.

"Steven gave it to me, he was waiting for me outside the washroom."

He looked at the money, then at her, his anger showing in his eyes. "I was wondering where he had taken off to." Then a thought hit him, holding the money up he snapped at her. "Oh my God, what did you do to earn two hundred dollars?"

She knew what he was getting at and it had her crying. "I didn't do anything, especially what you're insinuating, how could you even think I would?" She went to walk away but he grabbed her arm and held her.

"Then tell me, tell me why he would give you this money. I mean it Kiara, you tell me now or I'll take you right back now to America and hand you back over to the Sex Kittens."

She couldn't hold it back any longer, she started crying, talking through sobs. “Steven said not to tell you or he would destroy your reputation."

"I don't give a fuck what he said, tell me now."

"He knows you hired me from the Sex Kitten site." She then told him everything Steven said and did, even when they were at the wine tour and she showed him the sleeping pill she was supposed to give him. “If I give him a couple of hours he won't hurt you."

He tossed the money down on the bed and pulled her into his arms, hugging her. “I'm so sorry, you didn't deserve any of that. But you should never keep anything like that from me and he can't hurt me."

"If I don't show up at the hotel by ten he's going to tell everyone about us."

He pulled apart from her and placed his hands on each side of her face, wiping away her tears with his thumbs. "You're not going and he's not telling anyone." Letting go of her he picks up the money and starts walking out.

"Neil, where are you going?"

"I'm going to pay him a visit and give him back his money."

She put her hands on his arm. “I don't want you getting into trouble because of me."

"No need to worry about me, I can take care of myself. Now, where were you supposed to meet him and what is the room number?" It took some talking to get her to tell him and when she did he gave her a kiss before leaving.

He walked out of the hotel and walked around the corner to where Steven was waiting for Kiara, well he was in for one hell of a surprise. Five minutes after ten he knocked on the door to room 106. As soon as the door opened Steven's jaw dropped Neil pushed him back in, slamming the door shut behind him.

"Neil, what are you doing here," he asked, backing up.

"Who were you expecting?" he asked, giving him a shove back.

"Neil, hold on, it's not what said, holding up his hands. you think," he

"Oh really, then tell me what it is, is it Kiara you were expecting? You sick mother fucker, how dare you to try to force her to come here." He takes the money from his pocket and throws it in Steven's face. "I'm warning you, stay the fuck away from her and me. As long as you and I are friends that are over and never step foot in my hotel and casino ever again."

"Neil, when your time's up anyone can hire her and I plan on asking for her, she doesn't belong to you. I just wish I'd seen her profile before I spent all that money on those other whores."

His temper flared, the blood in his veins boiled, and charging Steven he grabbed him by the collar and shoved him up against the wall. "You listen to me you little slimeball, you'll not be calling and asking for her, if you try to I'll tell your wife how you've been going on that site and paying for sex. We both know if she finds out what you've been up to she'll divorce you and since it's her money that bought you the casino you'll lose everything. Do I make myself clear?"

He coughed, trying to breathe as he clawed at Neil's hands, trying to pry them off him. "Yes, it's clear," he said, choking.

He let go of him and backed away. "I thought we were friends but I didn't know what a sick fuck you were."

"I swear I'll stay away from her."

"Make sure you do," he said and walked over to the door, he knew Steven was following right behind him."

"Neil, I really don't understand why you are getting so worked up. She really is nothing but a dirty whore." He wished he had kept his mouth shut when Neil's fist connected with his face and he landed on his ass.

His hand was on the doorknob when Steven called her a whore, turning around he punched him, knocking him down. He towered over him, glaring angrily down at him. "Never call her that again or next time I'll do more than punch you," he said, turning he walked out and headed back to his hotel.

He was still so angry so he stopped at the bar before going up to his room and ordered a double scotch. He had never fought over a woman before, but hearing that man talk filth about her he lost his cool. It was then he realized that she meant more to him than just a sex kitten. Throwing money down for the drink he finished his scotch in one swallow and headed back to the room.

Chapter 6

She had changed into her nightgown, the one he had bought her, and was pacing back and forth, she worried sick about him. He had left here in a fit of anger and she was afraid of what he'd do to Steven. Then she heard the door open and turned her head, she watched as he closed it and he stood there staring at her. She ran over, jumped into his arms, and started sobbing as she wrapped her arms around his neck, resting her head against his. "I was so worried about you," she said through her sobs.

He wrapped his arms around her, his one hand stroking her hair in a loving gesture. "I'm fine and you don't have to worry about him, he's never going to bother you again. I told him if he even tried to get a date with you off the site I'll tell his wife what he's been up to."

She laid her head on his shoulder, she felt a sense of security being in his arms. “I hate that I put you in this situation."

"What situation?”

"Having to come to my rescue, causing you to fight with your friend."

He shifted her body to look at her. "None of this is your fault, Steven has always been a bit of a pervert. I really don't know why I was ever friends with him, we're not any longer. "Are you ready to go to bed?"

She nods and follows him when he takes her hand and they go into the bedroom. She helped him to remove his clothes, moving her hands slowly over his chest and shoulders. "I've not seen you work out so how did you get these muscles?" she asked, looking at his provocative lips.

"I find the time and what I want to do with you right now could be considered a workout," he said, pulling her nightgown up over her head.

She closed her eyes and arched her neck when he started kissing it, his shaft reared hot and hard against her. Her hands moved down his back to his ass, she loved how hard it was, every inch of him was so toned, sending shivers throughout her body. "Neil," she moaned his name when his hand went between her legs and his two fingers went inside her, stroking. She opened her eyes when he lifted her up and dropped her onto the bed.

"Tonight I am going to make you forget how that bastard treated you," he said, getting on top of her, and lowering his head to kiss her. It started off slow, his one hand thrusting his fingers inside her, feeling how wet she was. He took his time making love to her, making sure she was totally satisfied before he got his own release.

By the time he was done with her she was so exhausted, he tried out a couple of different positions on her, one of which really hit the G-spot, driving her wild. She went to sleep in his arms, forgetting all about what happened earlier.

The next few days flew by so quickly that they lost time, they went boating, to shows, to opera, and to long walks through the market square. She still hadn't told him much about herself, though he tried to get her to open up. But the more he pushed her the more she clammed up.

After today we only have two days left in Italy, is there anything or anywhere special you'd like to do or see?"

Wearing only a shirt over her bra and panties she goes over, her hand clutching his shirt she rested her head on his shoulder. The shirt was unbuttoned and had slid down past her shoulders. "You've shown me so much already, let's just stay in tonight."

Placing his hand on the wall, the other one in his pocket he smiled when she opened his shirt. "If we stay, what will we do to entertain ourselves?" He really liked it when she cuddled up to him, she was like a soft kitten, wanting affection from him.

"Let's take a bubble bath together," she said, kissing his neck.

"Wait, you want me, a man, to take a bubble bath?"

She traces his chin with her fingertips. "It'll be fun and very relaxing. I'll ride your torpedo," she said, placing her hand over his crotch. "We'll see if it's loaded and ready to fire," she said, giggling.

He looked down at her hand that was massaging his crotch and he smiled. "Well, in that case, you go ahead and start the bath, I'll be right in after I make a call." The swelling inside his pants grew hard, she really knew how to get him worked up.

When she left he made the call, checking to see how his business was doing. Satisfied that everything was running smoothly he hung up, removing his clothes as he made his way to the bathroom.

She was already in the tub when he walked in, dropping the remainder of his clothes onto the floor. "Come on in, the water is nice and warm," she said as she scooped up a handful of bubbles and rubbed them over her chest.

His mouth watered as he watched how her hands moved over her breasts and then circled the nipples with her fingers. He knew that she knew this action was getting him hot and excited, his cock was hard and standing at attention. He climbs into the tub and sitting down continues to watch her. Her eyes were closed, her head tilted back as she continued massaging her breasts.

She finally opened her eyes and saw the lust in his eyes, she could also see his manhood sticking up through the bubbles. "Do you want a turn?" she asked seductively. She let out a squeal when he grabbed her ankles and pulled her towards him.

"Damn right I do," he said, taking some bubbles in both hands and caressing her breasts with them. "Wrap your hand around my cock and play with it," he said, his breathing becoming ragged when she did what he asked.

"Oh looks like the torpedo is loaded," she said, feeling it throbbing in her hand. She held it firmly in her hand, moving it up and down. "It's so soft and really hard."

"It's loaded and ready to fire, now get on it and I'll prove it to you." He lifted her up and held on to her waist as he lowered her down onto his shaft till he had all of him inside her. He put his hand on the back of her head and pulled her in for a kiss, his hand on her breasts, running his thumb over the nipple.

With her hands on his shoulders, she started moving slowly up and down on him. When she saw him leaning back with his eyes closed and heard him tell her to go faster she did. "Oh God," she cried out when she felt an orgasm coming, the water from the tub splashed up and over the edge of the tub. She could feel him coming, felt his hands going around her waist, both grunting and moaning. Exhausted she leaned into him, his arms wrapping around her, stroking her back.

"Baby you were right, a bath is very relaxing."

Moving off him she turned around, her back resting against his chest as he wrapped his arms around her. "That felt so different from the other times, so good," she said, putting her hands over the top of his arms.

"There's a reason it felt different."

"What's that?" she asked, her eyes closed, lulled into a sense of contentment.

"I don't want you to freak out but we didn't use a condom."

She broke free from his arms and turned around to face him, her face white as a sheet. "No, oh what have we done? I can't get pregnant Neil, I just can't and I'm sure you don't want to be a father. What are we going to do?" she asked and started crying.

He pulled her back into his arms. "Don't cry, I know someone who can get us to plan B one step.

"What's that?" she asked, looking back at him.

"Most people know it as the morning-after pill, you take it and there won't be a baby."

"I'm so sorry, I never even thought to have a condom in here, it's all my fault."

"No, I'm as much to blame." He wiped her tears away. "Don't cry, I will fix it. Lay back and let's just calm down."

The water started getting cold so they got out and dried off. He went and made a call and after being assured that what he needed would be delivered shortly he poured them both a drink. They lay on the sofa together, falling asleep until someone knocks on the door, waking them up.

She stayed seated while he answered the door and watched as he spoke to the man and then gave him some money, taking the package from him. He then walked over and sat next to her, taking the item out of the bag. Handing her the glass of water that was on the table he takes the pill and hands it to her.

Taking the glass and the pill she looks at him, biting down on her bottom lip. "Is it safe to take?"

"Yes, it's perfectly safe and the man said the sooner you take it the better."

Nodding she pops it into her mouth and washes it down with the water. "I feel terrible about doing this but it's for the best. We can never forget to use protection again."

"We just got carried away, it won't happen again. Come on, let's go to bed, tomorrow we're going boating and then later to the ballet." He held her that night, feeling like a heel for not using protection and for her to take the pill. The timing was not right for him to become a father and he was sure she didn't want a baby.

"Even though I'm on the pill we can't forget to use a condom," she said, closing her eyes.

"Yes, the pill doesn't always work so it's better to use a condom for extra protection. We just got carried away, sorry. Don't you ever worry that your next client might not use one? God only knows what kind of disease he might give you." When he got no response from her he looked down and saw she had fallen asleep. He couldn't stand the thought of another man touching her but once their time was up he had no say in the matter.

The next morning he took her on a boat tour, then out to dinner, and after that went back to the hotel to get dressed for the ballet. He had bought her a long black sequin dress to wear and heels.

Going over placed his hands on her shoulders. "You're so beautiful, you take my breath away," he said, kissing her lips softly.

Before Neil had come into the bedroom she checked herself out in the mirror. The dress he had bought her was one she never thought she would ever be wearing. She was excited about going to the ballet and yet so sad as it meant this was going to be their last night together and he would be going back home. She wished that things could have been different, that she could stay with him but that was impossible. Going back to America and to those people was something she couldn't do. She forced a smile on her face when he entered the room and walked over to her, she closed her eyes when he kissed her.

He felt her arms tightening around him and he felt her body trembling, pulling back he looked into her eyes and saw tears. "What's wrong?"

How could she tell him that after tonight he'd never see her again? she couldn't. "It's nothing, I'm just overwhelmed. This dress is so beautiful, Italy and now going to the ballet. I've had the best time of my life with you."

"I feel the same way having you here with me. We still have all of tomorrow to go exploring before we head back the following day." He lifted her chin up. "No tears now or your mascara will start to run," he said jokingly. He sensed something was not right, that there was something she wasn't telling him. But he wanted her to enjoy the ballet and later he would make love to her, showing her how it really felt to be made love to, but tomorrow he would get right to the point and ask her to tell him everything about herself and what was going on.

Smiling back at him she takes his hand and they leave the hotel, getting into the cab that was waiting for them. The ballet was Romeo and Juliet. She sat holding his hand all through it, her eyes glued to the stage. "The music, the dancing, it's all so amazing.

I love it. Thanks for bringing me to see it. I will never forget it," she said, turning to smile at him.
With the show over, they went back to the hotel where he had a bottle of champagne chilling and poured them each a glass, handing her one.
"Tonight I am going to push your body to the limits, I am going to give you so much pleasure you'll forget your name but you will remember mine."

When they got back to the hotel she walked over to him, put her arms around his neck, reached up, and kissed him. Her kiss became more demanding, almost urgent. She wanted to have this one last night with him, to feel his touch and to know what it was like to be made love to by a good and decent man. She wanted to remember his kiss, his touch, knowing she would never see him again. "Neil, make love to me," she said, looking up at him when she broke the kiss.
There was something in the way that she looked at him and in her voice that sounded desperate, her eyes were tearing up. He cupped her face in his hands, rubbing his thumbs over her skin. He then pulled her face up and kissed her, his desire growing he picked her up in his arms and carried her to the bedroom.
Putting her down he turned her around so that he could pull down the zipper on her dress. He took his time as he kissed the back of her neck, sliding the straps of her gown past her shoulders, letting it fall into a pile by her feet. She wore no bra, his hands going around cupped her breasts in his

hands as he continued kissing her neck. He felt her arm going up and her hand touching the side of his head as she moaned softly.

Turning her around he lifted her up and laid her down on the bed. She lay there in only her panties, her chest rising and falling rapidly. Shedding his clothes as quickly as he could he got into bed and on top of her. Hands going on both sides of her face he lowered his lips onto hers, his kiss went deep, claiming her lips in a passionate kiss.

She traced her fingers up and down his back, loving how it felt having his naked body on top of her. Their skin was so warm touching was the best feeling she had ever felt, his hand between her legs, rubbing against her pussy had her whole body throbbing. She wanted him inside her, the need was so great she reached down and taking a hold of him put his hard cock inside her.

"Neil, I need you, take me now."

He didn't need her to say it, he wanted her as much as she wanted him. Kissing her he began to thrust into her, feeling her heat over his shaft as her walls clamped down around him. Her legs were around him, her arms holding onto him as he started thrusting harder and faster inside her. His muscles flexed, tightening as he rode her until he heard the sweet moans coming from her luscious lips then he too came. Breathing heavily, his heart racing, and drops of sweat fell from his forehead he collapsed, his full weight laying on top of her.

Knowing he was about to roll off her she tightens her hold on him, her arms refusing to let him leave.

"Don't move off me yet," she said, kissing his shoulder.

He sensed a sadness about her, it felt almost like she was trying to tell him something. It felt like goodbye. Putting his weight on his elbows he looked down at her. "You look so sad, there's no need to be sad, we still have a week together after we get back home."

She moved her hands over his shoulder. "I know, it's just that these past three weeks have been amazing. I've had the best time of my life and I want you to know that I enjoyed every minute with you. I'll never forget you or how tender and kind you treated me." A sob broke free and she looked at his chest, not wanting to look into his eyes. "I hope you don't forget me."

"I'll never forget you," he said, lowering his head and kissing her before rolling off and onto his side, pulling her close. "Quit that job, it's not for you. I can give you a job in my hotel or the casino, the pay is good."

She laid her head on his chest. "I'm tired, can we talk later?" she asked, knowing she wouldn't be here when he woke.

"OK, we will continue this conversation tomorrow," he said, closing his eyes. He was determined to get her to quit the site and find a less degrading job, so he closed his eyes and went to sleep.

She lay awake, listening to him breathing and the hum from the alarm clock. Earlier she had slipped out from under his arm and watched him, the tears that fell from her eyes made her pillow wet. When she knew he was deeply asleep she moved as quietly as she could and got out of bed. She started dressing into the jeans and top that were laying on the chair next to the bed, keeping her eyes on him to make sure he wasn't waking up.

Slipping into the jacket she walks to the door, stopping to look back at him, the tears falling freely down her face. She knew she had fallen in love with him but she couldn't stay, he didn't love her and there was no way she could go back to America. "I'm so sorry Neil, goodbye," she said quietly under her breath.

Earlier that day when he had gone out she packed a small bag with just a few clothes and had it hidden under the cabinet in the kitchen. Taking it out and making sure she didn't make any noise went to the front door. His wallet was laying on the small table along with the car keys. Picking up the wallet she opens it and takes out the wad of cash that was there. She left him a note saying she was sorry. Just as she turned the doorknob and the door opened a crack it slammed shut, she gasped and looked up at a very angry man.

"Are you going somewhere?" he asked, then saw the money in her hand. "And you're stealing from me."

"Neil, I'm sorry."

He grabs the money and throws it down where it is scattered everywhere. "Why are you sneaking away in the middle of the night and how can you steal from me after everything I've done for you? Well, you're not going anywhere lady."

"Neil, keep the money, just let me go," she said between sobs.

Seeing her cry and how scared she was, his anger went away, and he held onto her shoulders. "Kiara, you have to tell me what you are so scared of, who are you running away from?"

She shook her head, refusing to look at him. "I can't tell you. Don't make me go back there, to them."

He shook her, making her look at him. "Let me help you."

"You can't help me, no one can," she said, looking at him.

"Yes I can, but only if you tell me everything." He cupped her face in his hands. "You have to trust me."

"It's a long story," she answered, her body slouching.

"Let's sit down and I'll pour us both a stiff drink." Taking her hand led her over to the sofa, making her sit down. He then went and poured them both a shot of whiskey. Normally he wouldn't give her the hard stuff but he figured she needed something stronger than beer or wine. "Now start from the beginning."

"When my mother died I found myself homeless, living on the streets. At times I stayed in shelters when there was a spot available. I was working as a waitress but lost it because my mother would show up there high, causing a scene, before she died of course. I met this guy, Charlie, he was so nice and he took me to get something to eat. We talked and he offered me a place to stay. Living on the streets was so scary so I thought staying with him was better and I moved in with him. We soon became close and started having a relationship. It was good for a while until one day he brought another man home and said they wanted to do a threesome. When I refused Charlie kicked me out and I was once again on the streets." She finished her drink and asked for another one.

He got up and poured her a drink but watered it down, knowing she wasn't used to hard liquor.

"I had only gotten a few blocks when a dark van pulled up beside me and the side door opened and two men grabbed me and shoved me inside. My hands were tied up, my eyes were covered with a blindfold. Something was put over my mouth and the next thing I knew I woke up in a cell, chained to the wall in just my bra and panties."

He felt his body tensing, his hand gripping his glass, he had a feeling where this was going and he didn't like it. "I know this is hard, but please, go on."

"There were other women there, girls really, some no older than fifteen. For two days I watched the girls come and go. We were beaten, and starved, with nothing to keep us warm. I heard stories about how the ones who refused to do what they were told were never seen again. I found out that these men kidnapped girls who had no one looking for them, ones who had no families who would miss them. They sold some of the girls outright, others they put to work on their kitten site."

Neil ran his hand over his face. "My God, human trafficking. I swear I never for one minute thought this was what it was. I honestly thought it was just a dating site. I knew there could be sex involved but never thought it was forced."

"I saw them kill one young girl right in front of me when she told them to go to hell, that she would never do what they wanted. On my third night there I was taken into another room where a man was waiting for me. I thought he was going to rape me but he just wanted to talk. He gave me a choice, either I join the site and do as I was told or they would sell me. I knew they wouldn't kill me because if they did they wouldn't be able to make any money off me."

"So you agreed to do it," he said, feeling bad for her.

"I was scared, I knew what they were capable of doing. They cleaned me up, had my hair and nails done and waxed me down there, and warned me to keep it that way. My picture was taken and put up on the site. I had only been up maybe an hour before you and some others put a bid up, I guess you lg were the highest. "Lucky for me," she said, looking at him with tears in her eyes.

He went and sat next to her, putting his arms around her.

"I was told to do whatever the client wanted, and if I disappointed you in any way or told you the truth they would kill me and you, the client. So you see I couldn't tell you anything, I took a chance telling you what little I did. When you told me we were coming here I planned on running away, knowing they would never find me here."

He stroked her hair as she cried on his shoulder. "You could have told me. I would have done something to help you, I would have understood."

"Just let me go and when you go back home you can tell them I ran away. Just call them and act like you're furious, I know you can convince them you know nothing."

"People like that are dangerous, they will send someone to find you. It's better you come back with me."

She tore out of his arms. “If I go back they'll come for me and God only knows who they will send me to next. I can't, I can't let another man touch me, not after being with you."

He grabbed her arms. "We still have a week left together when we go back. I promise I'll think of a way to get you out of this situation. I'm not going to let them get their hands on you, you have to trust me, do you?”

Her eyes were red and swollen from crying, she looked at him, taking a deep breath. "Yes, I trust you." She looked him right in the eye. "I trust you with my life." She meant it, her gut told her that if anyone could keep her safe and get her out of this mess it was him.

He gave her a tender kiss. "Let's go to bed and get some sleep. We still have one more day left here so what would you like to do?"

"I just want to stay in," she said, feeling emotionally exhausted.

"Then that's what we'll do, room service and a day in bed."

"Neil, there is one more thing that I've been keeping from you and you have a right to know. I just hope you'll not be mad.

He pinched the bridge of his nose, worried about what he was going to hear next. "Alright, lay it on me."

Chapter 7

She was nervous about telling him, thinking he would be upset but he had a right to know. "I'm not twenty-two, I'm only nineteen." She waited for him to explode, to rant but he didn't.

He got up and ran his hand through his hair as he started pacing back and forth. "Shit, nineteen, eight years younger than me. That's not so bad, you're still of legal age." He went and sat down next to her. "I'm glad you told me."

"You're not mad?" she asked.

"You're younger than I would have liked, but no, I'm not mad." He put his arms back around her, holding her close to him. "I promise I'll get you away from those bastards, let's go back to bed."

As she lay in his arms, she stared up at him. "I really am sorry about taking that money from your wallet. I have never stolen money before and I felt terrible about doing it. Can you forgive me?"

"I know you were just desperate so there's nothing to forgive."

The next day they spent inside, going out later to take a swim in the pool and later ordered room service.

"I wish we could stay here like this forever," she said that night after making love.

"Me too, but my life is back in Las Vegas," he said, holding her until she went to sleep. He stayed awake trying to think of what he was going to do to get her out of that business and away from those people. When he woke up she was still in his arms, he had always liked his space in bed but for some reason, he didn't mind having her sleep in his arms.

She opened her eyes and smiled up at him. "Morning," she said, her lips going to his neck she started kissing, moving down to his chest. With his hard, warm skin against hers, she got turned on, her core throbbing and pussy wet she climbed on top of him. "How soon do we have to get ready to catch our flight?"

"We have plenty of time for what you've got in mind," he said, and flipping her over onto her back he was now the one on top. "This will have to be quick," he said, not wasting any time getting inside her.

Once they were seated on the plane she leaned back and looked out the window. "I'm going to miss Italy." She turned to him. "I really do thank you for bringing me here. Everything was perfect, the people, the food, all of it."

"You were perfect," he said, taking her hand and kissing it. "I've been thinking about your situation and a week isn't long enough to come up with a plan to get you away from those people. So I'm going to call the site and tell them I want to book you for another month."

"Neil, I already told you they won't do that, they don't want the client and kitten bonding and getting close."

He rubbed his chin, trying to think of something else. "I got it, I'll have my friend Eric call and hire you for the month."

"You want me to be Eric's sex kitten?"

He grabbed her hand when she pulled away. "Not the way you think. I'll get him to book you and you'll still be with me, only they'll think you're with the new client. It will give me more time to figure things out."

"What makes you think he'll do it?"

"We're friends, once I explain what's going on he'll help us. Look, I don't want you to worry, everything is going to work out, I promise."

They were both tired by the time the plane landed and were glad to get back to his hotel. As soon as they walked in the front door to the lobby he was approached by a couple of his employees who wanted to talk with him.

"You go on up to the suite, I'll join you soon." He turned to the clerk and instructed him to have someone go up with her and carry the bags.

He had just gotten there as she came from the shower. She was wrapped in a towel, her hair still wet with droplets of water dripping down her shoulders onto her breasts. His eyes glinted in them as he walked over to her. "You are in grave danger right now."

"Who from?" she asked, her eyes growing wide when she looked at him.

"From me," he answered, tearing off her towel and pushing her down on the bed. He smiled at her while he quickly removed his clothes. Getting into bed he got on top of her, his lips going to hers as he moved his hand over her body. After satisfying both of their lust they got dressed and she made them something to eat while he made a call to Eric, asking him to come over.

They were just finishing their meal when there was a loud knock at the door. "That will be Eric," he said, getting up and walking into the other room and letting him in.

"How was your trip?" Eric asked, sitting down and taking the drink Neil offered him.

"It was really good, we had a great time."

"So what was so important that I had to rush over?"

Just then Kiara came into the room and sat down next to him. She said hello, but being shy around Eric she kept quiet and let the men talk.

"Eric, I need you to do something for me, it's really important."

"Anything pal, just name it."

"I want you to go on the sex kitten site and hire Kiara for a month when my time is up."

Eric looked from him to her and back again. "Wait a minute, you told me I couldn't do that when I mentioned it and now you want her to be with me."

Neil shook his head. "No, not like that, I just want you to book her. I would do it myself but they won't allow it. She'll be staying with me, you just have to be the one to ask for her. I will give you the money, it's not going to cost you a dime."

"But why? I don't get it."

He explained to Eric how it was a human trafficking site and how the girls were forced to work for them. He told him everything that Kiara had told him. "I need time to figure out a way to get her away from them and possibly have them shut down."

Eric sat back, shaking his head. "Shit, it makes me sick thinking of those poor girls being forced into sex slavery. You say some of the girls are as young as fourteen?" he asked, looking at her.

"Yes, I was one of the lucky ones. I had just been put up and Neil was my first client. I wasn't there long enough to have gotten raped, just starved and beaten for a couple of days. I could have ended up with someone who would have abused me." She looked at Neil but was talking to Eric. "He was good to me, kind, he never hurt me."

"Give me your laptop, I'll do it now."

"No, you should use your own, just in case they figure out it came from the same computer, we don't want them catching on to what we're up to."

"How high are you willing to go?"

"Give them whatever they ask for. As soon as you hear from them, call me and I'll transfer the money into your account. Be careful with these people, they're dangerous. If you don't want to do this I will understand. I have no idea what's going to happen and I hate to put you in danger."

"I've got your back Neil and besides, I can take care of myself. I'll go home now and get started, we wouldn't want someone outbidding us." He stands up and looks at her. "We'll get you out of this mess."

"Thank you," she said, feeling so grateful to him.

After he left they sat back down. "What happens now?" she asked, taking a hold of his hand.

"We wait for Eric to call us and tomorrow we'll go to the police station and tell them about the site."

She jumped up, staring down at him, fear made her body shake. "We can't do that. If they find out I talked to the cops they'll kill me and you too. My God Neil, you and your whole family will be in danger. These monsters won't think twice about killing you, or your niece. No, I won't put you all in danger."

"Judy's husband is an FBI agent, he can investigate them and have them shut down and put in prison. He can also protect his family, we have to tell him, not just for you but for all those girls who are kept and used as sex slaves, think of them."

"Your brother-in-law is a cop? You never told me that and I was in his home."

"It never came up. Maybe it would be best if I had him come here and tell him what's going on, that way no one will see you going to the station, we'll let him handle it. Kiara, it's the only way, they have to be stopped."

Trembling with fear she let him hold her.

"I'll call him tomorrow after Eric has secured the deal. I'm not sure how this will work, but I want to make sure you're with me when it all goes down."

She looked up at him, her lips quivering. "Why are you doing this for me?"

"Don't you know?" he asked, touching her cheek in a loving gesture.

She shakes her head.

"It's because I have fallen in love with you."

"I love you too," she said through her tears. "I had fallen in love with you just before we left for Italy. But I never dreamed that you would ever love me, I thought I was nothing but a prostitute to you."

"I told you once before never to talk about yourself in that way. You were kidnapped and forced to go along with their demands, you are a victim. I know people, and I know you are a good person." His arms wrapped around her, and his kiss was hot and passionate as he lifted her up and laid her down on the sofa.

They removed each other's clothes slowly, their hands and lips exploring every inch of the other one's body. He moved inside her, making her squirm and moan. It felt so good, better than before and maybe that was partly because they had raw sex, and the condom was forgotten. He could have stopped, or she could have but neither one wanted to.

They stayed on the sofa, he covered them with the throw that hung over the back. She laid on top of him, her head on his chest. They ended up sleeping there until morning, he woke first and carefully rolled her onto her back, making sure not to wake her. Covering her up he went to shower and change, he had to go downstairs and tend to business. He left her a note, saying where he was, and told her not to open the door for anyone. Giving her a kiss on top of her head he left his suite.

Waking up she smiled when she read his note, she was already missing him but she also knew he had a business to run. Dropping the cover she goes and takes a shower, she was shocked to see all the love bites that covered her breasts and inner thighs. A smile crossed her face just thinking about how passionate and intense his lovemaking was. Every inch of her felt sore, it was a wonder she was able to get up and walk.

He had been gone for hours and she was getting bored, so she thought she would go down and see if he was in his office. She was hoping they could have lunch together. Putting on one of the dresses he bought her she went down. Going straight to his office she knocked before entering but he wasn't there. Leaving his office she went to the front desk and asked the person behind the desk if they knew where he was. No one knew so after an hour of looking for him she went back up to his suite.

"Where the fuck have you been?"

She jumped when she saw him and heard him yelling. "I went down to your office to see if you wanted lunch."

He grabbed her arm and shook her. "Don't ever do that again."

"Do what?" she asked, tears springing to her eyes. She didn't like this side of him and it scared her. "Let go, you're hurting me," she cried out.

He released her and stepped back. "You scared the fucking shit out of me. I came back and you weren't here. I thought something happened to you, that maybe they came and took you." Seeing her close to tears he felt bad and needed to explain. "Kiara, until we know you are in no danger you can't go wandering around on your own. Anything could have happened to you. Promise me you won't leave this room again unless I'm with you."

"I didn't think anything would happen as long as they knew you still had me for another week. I'm tired of having to stay inside, I was bored. I only wanted to have lunch with you," she said, sniffling.

He pulled her into his arms, his hand cupping the side of her face. His eyes held worry and concern. "I'm sorry I left you alone for so long. I'll order us some room service and spend the rest of the day with you. Tomorrow you can come with me when I go back down." He lowered his lips and kissed her.

That night they were cuddled up on a blanket on the sofa watching the news when his phone rang. Picking it up, I looked at the caller id, seeing it was Eric, and he answered. After several minutes he hung up. "That was Eric, the site got back to him, and it's all set. I just have to transfer the money into his account," he said and got up he went over to his computer and started punching the keys. "There, all done," he said out loud, closing the computer he went back over to her.

"I feel terrible that you are spending all this money because of me."

He put his arm around her, pulling her back against him. "It's only money. They did double the amount though, the greedy bastards. Do they at least give any of the money to the women?"

"No. They just kept them as animals in between jobs." cages like

"I called Roy, he's coming over later."

"Already? I didn't think you were going to say anything to him until later."

"The sooner he gets on the case the quicker it'll be over. I know you're scared but we can trust Roy."

An hour later Roy showed up and greeted her with a friendly smile and a quick hug. "OK, you didn't give me much to go on over the phone, so let's hear everything." He sat there, taking the drink that Neil handed him. He listened, not saying anything, making notes on his pad, and after they told him every little detail that was when he started speaking.

"There are many of these sites out there, most are legit dating sites. Human trafficking ones are hard to find and prove. These people are smart, they know as long as they don't specify that the women are for sex they can get away with it."

"But they do advertise that the women will do anything you want them to do," Neil said, feeling frustrated.

"I know, but they can claim they're talking about going places, pretending to be a girlfriend, etc. I will get my team together and we'll start checking them out. Bringing these people down will take time, weeks, months, sometimes years."

"Damn it, Roy, we don't have that much time. I got Eric to hire her for the month, thinking that would be enough time. I can't let them take her when the time is up, I won't. She told you what all she saw, the killing, beatings, what more do you need?"

"Neil, I promise I'll make it my priority. If worse comes to worst we'll put her in the witness protection program."

"What?" she asked, staring at Roy.

"Kiara, you are a witness and will have to testify in court. Once this is blown open and there's a chance they'll know it was you who snitched on them and they will come after you, your life will be in danger. It's the only way to keep you safe and alive. But I don't want you to worry, nothing is going to take place until I find out more about the site and the ones who own and run it."

She felt Neil's hand on her knee and looked at him. "I didn't know I had to face them in court, I'm really scared." She was hoping that once they were caught with all the women they had chained up the girls would tell the cops everything that would be the end of it.

"Kiara, try not to worry, let me work on this and when I know more we'll go from there. I better get home now, Judy's waiting for me."

"You're not going to tell her about this are you?" Neil asked, getting to his feet. The last thing he needed was for his sister to know.

"We never discuss my cases until it's all over, then I will have to tell her. She's going to give you hell. I'll get back to you as soon as I find anything out. You also did good by getting Eric to hire her for the month, at least here we'll know she's safe."

"I'll walk you out," he said and followed Roy over to the door and went into the hallway with him, he wanted to talk to him without her hearing.

"So, what you told me and Judy that night when you came for dinner was all lies. I have to say I'm a little surprised that you went on a dating site to get a girl."

"Roy, it was just a spur-of-the-moment thing but it's a good thing I did."

"Yes, yes it was. Neil, are you in love with her?"

"I am. I only wanted her as a companion when I went to Italy, and yes sex was also part of it. But something happened, and without meaning to I fell hard for her. Kiara is a beautiful and sweet girl. I didn't know she was only nineteen, but that doesn't matter."

"I thought so. Keep her close and if there are any problems call me. One more thing, it may come down to her having to go into hiding, which means you won't get to see her. How do you feel about that?"

"I'm hoping it doesn't come to that but if it does I'll go with her."

"What about your business?"

"I have people that will take care of it. There's no way I'm letting her go without me, I can help keep her safe."

"From what she has told us these people are dangerous, they won't think twice about killing anyone who tries to take them down. Watch your back and don't do anything foolish, let us who are trained take them down."

He smiled. "You know me, now what could I do?"

"I do know you, just don't try to play the hero. See you later bro."

He went back inside and found her drinking scotch, and coughing. Going over he took it from her and went and got her a glass of wine. "Here, drink this instead, you know you can't handle the hard stuff." He brushed a strand of hair that had fallen over her eye. "I know you're scared but I won't let anything happen to you. If things get bad and they put you in protective custody I'll be going with you."

She looked up at him. "You will?"

"I love you, do you really think I'd let you go without me?"

"But we could be gone for a long time, what about your business?"

"To hell with the business, from now on my job is to make sure you're safe. I've never felt this way about any other woman before." He lifted her chin up. "For the first time in my life, I've thought of someone else besides myself. I now know what Judy has been telling me for years about love, she was right. She told me when the right woman came along I'd know it, and baby, you are here. I love you." He lowered his mouth onto hers, his kiss tender, loving.

The next few days went way too fast and it was almost time when they would be picking her up to take her over to the next client, Eric. She was packed and her bags by the door, she ran into his arms, letting him hold her.

"It's going to be alright, I'll come and get you by three in the morning."

"Why so late?" she asked, sniffling.

"I just want to be sure they aren't watching Eric's place." He lifted her head up, his fingers under her chin. "They're going to be here any minute. Stay strong and just keep your head down. I hate letting you leave with them, it's killing me."

Just then there was a loud knocking at the door.

"I want you to listen to me, don't be upset with what I might have to say in front of them, just know I don't mean any of it, I love you." He pulled her into his arms, kissing her long and hard, pouring all of his love for her into that kiss before letting her go."

"I love you," she said quietly before he opened the door.

He opened the door and stared at the two men who were standing there, one was the same guy that had brought her to him, and the other one he hadn't seen before. He put his hands in his pocket so that they wouldn't see how his hands were balled up into fists.

"We're here for the girl," the one said, removing his dark sunglasses. "Did she give you any trouble?"

"No, she was a good girl, the bitch did everything I told her to do." He felt like shit calling her that and hoped she wouldn't hate him. "In fact, I'd like to hire her again."

"We have plenty of other girls, even better than this one, try one of them next time." The man cleared his throat and neither man moved.

"Did you want something?" Neil asked.

"Most clients give the girls a small tip for their, hum, services."

Neil pulled out his wallet and took out five one hundred crisp bills. going over to her he folded the money and stuck his hand down her top, sticking the money in her bra. He felt her heart beating fast against his hand. "Here you go, doll face, you were the best lay I've had in a long time."

"Thank the man," the big one said, grabbing her by the arm and giving her a shake.

Seeing the man grabbing her he wanted to kill him and thought maybe someday he might get the chance.

She looked up at him and could see how sorry he was. "Thank you, sir," she said and lowered her head again.

Neil wanted to pull her away from the man and beat the shit out of them. Instead, he bit his tongue and kept quiet. It tore him in half when they walked away with her and he closed the door. He went and phoned Eric, letting him know they had picked her up and would be bringing her to him. He also said to call him back as soon as they left his place. He started pacing back and forth, keeping an eye on his watch. He estimated that she should be at Eric's place within an hour.

As soon as the three of them were in the elevator and the door closed the big one put his hands around her throat and pinned her up against the wall. He then put his hand down her top and took out the money, holding it up he turned to the other guy.

"That guy was a good tipper," he said, and releasing her he put the money in his pocket.

She clutched the top of her blouse, holding it shut and feeling sick to her stomach from his touch on her skin. She didn't like the way they were looking at her and it was making her sick hearing what they were saying about her. She kept her eyes down as she listened to them, wishing she was with Neil.

"The whore must be really good for that guy to dish out so much money for her. We could each take a turn with her before we deliver to the next guy." The smaller one of the two said as he eyed her up and down.

The bigger one stared at her. “As much as I would like to fuck the bitch we have strict orders to take her straight to the other client." He then laughed. "But I promise you when we go back for her we'll take her to my place and have some fun with her before we put her back in her cage."

"She must be good if all these guys are booking her for a month each time, we are going to make a bundle off her."

"Yeah I know, this last one paid double what the other one did. We might even get quite a bit for her when she gets older and is no longer popular with the clients."

"She has a few years left in her before we have to sell her."

The bigger one looked at her. "You didn't tell that guy anything did you?"

"No," she answered, shaking her head.

"Keep it that way if you want to live, and want the client to live too."

When they got to the van they shoved her inside and the smaller one opened up her suitcase and searched through it. "Nothing here, it's all clean," he said, picking up a pair of her panties he smelled. "Smells nice, I bet your pussy does too."

She turned her head away, not wanting to see the ugly smirk on his face. She thanked God that they had to take her straight to Eric's, otherwise she knew they would have raped her. Some of the other girls would talk, saying how they took turns with them, then making them bathe before being taken to a client.

The smaller one drove while the bigger one rode in the back with her. They drove for almost an hour before the driver parked the van and she was pulled out of the van. Both men walked on either side of her, the one had a strong hold on her arm while the other one carried her case.

Chapter 8

The smaller guy, we'll call him Frank, knocked on Eric's door, while they waited for him to answer the bigger one yanked her arm. "Remember the rules, keep your mouth shut and do whatever he wants."

The door opened and Eric smiled. "Yes, my kitten has finally arrived," he said, rubbing his hands together, and then stepping aside to let them enter. He looked at her, put his hand under her chin, and lifted her head up. "You are much prettier in person. We are going to be really good at doing bad things together." He noticed the red mark around her neck and knew if Neil saw it he would flip out.

"Sign here," Frank said when he handed Eric the form. "If you have any trouble with her just call us and we'll come back and have a few words with her."

Eric laughed. "There won't be any need for that, I know how to handle these bitches," he said, putting his fingers on his belt, letting the men know what he meant.

Once the men had left and he shut the door he turned to look at her. "Kiara, I'm so sorry, I hope you know that what I said was just an act. Come on and sit down. Would you like something to drink?"

She shook her head and went and sat on the sofa.

"Just relax, Neil wanted me to call him the moment you got here." He got on his phone and started talking to him. "Calm down man, she just got here and she's alright, yup, hang on," he said and handed her the phone. "He wants to talk to you."

"Neil," she said, taking the phone. It had only been just a little over an hour but already she was missing him. "I miss you so much. No, I'm alright but do you have to wait so long to get me?" She listened to him talk for a few minutes. "I love you too," she said before handing the phone back to Eric.

After a few words with Neil, he hung up and sat across from her. "We're going to be here for a few hours. Are you hungry? I could heat up some leftovers or order in takeout."

"I'm not hungry," she answered, looking around the apartment.

"Kiara, when I first found out that he called that site and you showed up I thought the worse about you. But knowing you and how Neil feels about you I know now how wrong I was. I'm sorry for what you've been through but he will help you. The guy is crazy in love with you, he's never felt this way before."

She looked at him, her eyes were scratchy from crying. "He's the kindest man I've ever met and when I'm with him I feel so safe. I never believed in love until I met him, but I'm hopelessly in love with him."

"I can see that, now let's have a drink. I have beer and wine, which would you prefer?"

"I wouldn't mind a beer," she answered. He was being so nice to her and she started to relax a little.

He got up and left the room, bringing back two beers, one he had put in a glass for her. "So what shall we do? We can play cards, watch TV or just talk." He couldn't help liking her, she was so sweet and he understood how Neil fell in love with her so quickly.

"Let's talk, tell me how you two met."

"Neil and I go way back, since high school and we've been friends ever since. I was the nerd but he was the popular one. He played football and had lots of girlfriends but he was a good guy, nice to everyone. We went to college together and shared a dorm room. I even had a crush on Judy at one time but he was so protective of her and told me to stay away from her."

"If you liked her he really had no right to tell you that."

"In a way he did, I was kind of a player once we went to college. Making up for my high school years. Anyways she met Roy and they fell deeply in love so it all worked out."

"Is there no one in your life now?" she asked. She was curious about the man Neil seemed to trust.

"I haven't found the right one yet, but I'm still hoping. If Neil can find love then there's hope for me. Hey, you want some pizza?"

She smiled, feeling more at ease with him and the thought of pizza sounded good. "I could eat some."

He ordered the pizza and while they waited he got them another beer and they talked some more. He told her more about himself and some of the antics he and Neil had gotten into over the years. Pizza came and after eating they turned on the TV.

"I'm sorry you have to stay and babysit me, I'm sure you'd rather be out with a woman and having some fun," she said, yawning. Though she felt bad about him having to give up his night to stay with her she was still glad that she wasn't alone.

"I had no plans for tonight, besides I'm enjoying your company. You're tired," he said when he saw her yawn. "If you like you can go lay down on my bed and get some sleep before Neil picks you up." He could see she was having trouble keeping her eyes open.

"I'm alright. I don't want to take your bed, I'll just lay my head down here. You really don't have to stay with me, you can go to bed."

"Don't be silly, I have to wait up for Neil. Come with me and I'll show you where the bedroom is," he said, waiting for her to follow him. "You should be comfortable here and don't worry, as soon as Neil gets here I'll wake you."

"Thank you, maybe I will rest for a little while." When he left she laid down, she felt drained and it wasn't long before she drifted off to sleep.

Eric had just dozed off when he heard the knock, getting up he goes over and opens the door and finds Neil there wearing jeans and a hoodie. "What are you wearing?" he asked, snickering, and then noticed the other hoodie in his hand.

"I didn't want anyone to recognize me, where's Kiara?" he asked, walking in and looking around.

"She's in my bed."

Neil swung around to look at Eric, he lowered his brow, and his nostrils flared. "You son of a bitch, what did you do to her?" he asked, grabbing him by the collar.

"Holy shit, I didn't do anything to her," he said, pulling his hands away. "Damn man, calm down. She was falling asleep so I told her to go lay down on my bed. You know I wouldn't try anything with your girl."

"Eric, I'm sorry. I've just been a nervous wreck since she left."

"She's asleep right now so let me pour you a drink before you wake her up." He walked over to his mini bar and taking out a bottle of whiskey poured them both a shot.

"How was she when those men brought her here, did they harm her?"

"Well, the big ugly one had a tight grip on her arm and she did have a mark around her neck but it faded, she looked scared as shit. We had a nice long talk and I see now how you fell in love with her, she's super sweet."

"I never intended on falling in love, it just happened," he said, finishing off his drink.

They both turned their heads when they heard her enter the room and called out.

Hearing voices coming from the other room she sat up, rubbing the sleep from her eyes that were still scratchy from crying. It was Neil's voice she heard so jumping off the bed hurried out of the room and seeing him she called out his name. When he turned to her she ran into his arms, letting him lift her up as he wrapped his arms tightly around her.

"God baby, I've been worried sick about you." He sat her down and cupping her face in his hands he kissed her, it was a deep and passionate kiss, not caring that they had an audience. “Let's get you home,” he said when he finally pulled away. "Put this on," he said, handing her the hoodie.

"Neil, you know once you get back to your place it might not be a good idea to be seen with her, in case they happen to see you together," Eric said as he watched the way they were with each other.

"Shit, I never thought of that." He looked at her, placing his hands on her shoulders. "He's right, we can't be seen together. It might be best if you stay here and I can come to see you."

"What? no way," she cried out.

“Kiara, if you come with me you'll have to stay hidden inside my suite the whole time. You won't be able to go out by the pool or the restaurants or shopping."

"I don't care, I'm staying with you," she said. Burying her head in his chest she started sniffling.

"You'll be bored to death," he said, his hand stroking her head.

"I won't be bored. I'll clean, cook, watch TV and read. I'll keep busy, just let me go home with you." She looked up at him. “I was chained up to a wall in a cold damp cell, I know I can handle staying inside a luxury hotel suite."

"Alright," he said, giving in. Before leaving he turned to Eric. "Try and keep a low profile in case they are watching you. Oh, and they might call you in a couple of days to see how things are going. If they ask to talk to her, make up an excuse as to why she can't come to the phone."

"Neil, I got this, don't worry about a thing," Eric said as he walked them over to the door.

When she put on the hoodie he pulled the hood up over her head. As soon as the elevator doors closed he pulled her into his arms, placing his lips on hers. He couldn't wait to get her home, she would be safer there than out here in the open. He let out a sigh of relief when they left the building and got into his vehicle without anyone around.

She moved over closer to him as he drove and she liked when he put his arm around her shoulders.

"Eric said you had a mark on your neck, did one of them do that to you?"

Leaning her head on his shoulder she started telling him what went down. "One of them put their hand around my throat and took the money out of my bra. They searched my luggage and the smaller one said they should take turns with me before delivering me to Eric. I was so scared, I thought they were actually going to do it. The other one said they didn't have time but said when the month was up they would have some fun with me before taking me back to the agency."

He felt the rage boiling in his veins. The thought of how those men treated her and what they wanted to do he hoped that someday he'd be able to beat the shit out of them. "They aren't going to get near you again, I'll make sure of it."

Making it back to his place without being seen they went to the bedroom, getting undressed they got into bed. Even though it was late they both wanted, more like needed each other. Their kisses became more passionate as he climbed on top of her and entered her after finding how wet she was.

"Neil, don't you want to use protection?"

"You're still taking the pill aren't you?" he asked, stopping what he was doing to look at her. He knew she had used protection when she was with her ex, and he also always used condoms so he knew they were both clean.

"Yes," she answered.

He touched her face lovingly. "I know when we had unprotected sex in Itlay I had you take the morning-after pill but it was different between us then. I only had you take it for extra protection but now I don't see the need for condoms. But if you want me to put one on I will."

She liked the feel of his cock uncovered inside her, it felt hard and velvety. Thinking back to that night and how much better it felt she traced his lips with her fingers. “No, I don't want you to put one on, it's so much better without one."

He smiled and started thrusting, going deep and watching her face when he went faster, loving the sounds of her moans. There wasn't a lot of foreplay, but their lovemaking was tender and sweet.

They slept until noon, he ignored the phone when it rang and he turned the volume way down so as not to disturb them. But he also knew that he would have to get up and make an appearance downstairs soon. Turning his head he looked at her and his heart skipped a beat. She looked so innocent, so sweet. Not being able to control himself he got on top of her and leaning down kissed her until he felt her responding.

She felt his weight on her and his lips on hers, eyes still closed she kissed him back, putting her arms around him. Swept away in a frenzy of wild sex she squirmed and moaned loudly when he brought her to the most amazing orgasm. It was exciting to hear how much he enjoyed it, his moans and his whispering her name in her ear got her wetter than she was already.

He rolled off her, taking her hand and placing it over his heart. "Do you feel that? You do this to me, you have my heart beating so hard it feels like it's going to burst right out of my chest."

"Mine too," she said, putting her head on his chest, her fingers caressing him.

"I would love to stay in bed with you all day but it's already past noon. Make me some coffee while I take a shower if you don't mind."

She not only made coffee but also eggs and toast.

After he ate he kissed her before leaving for work. "Don't answer the door for anyone. I'll just be downstairs. If you need me just call and I'll be right here," he said, handing her a phone. "My number is on the speed dial. I'll try not to be too late. I love you."

She kept busy cleaning and she made a pot roast for dinner, hoping he'd be home soon. She decided to surprise him by wearing just one of his shirts over her bra and panties. It always seems to get him excited when she wore one of his shirts which would lead to some really hot sex.

Neil was a wreck all afternoon, all he could think about was her being alone up in his suite. He knew he was whipped, she had him by the balls, in more ways than one. He did what had to be done, greeting some of his high rollers, making sure the staff was keeping the guests happy, and finishing up some work in his office. He looked at the time and seeing it was seven o'clock decided to call it a day.

Walking into his suite the aroma of meat reached him and he smiled, it was pot roast, his favorite. "I'm back baby," he shouted out as he walked towards the kitchen. He stopped in the doorway and took a deep breath. "Shit," he swore when he saw her wearing just a shirt, and when she turned around he noticed it was unbuttoned, and under it were her black bra and panties. He felt his manhood getting hard, damn, this woman was going to be the death of him.

"Hi," she said smiling when she saw him. "I made your favorite, I was hoping you'd be home soon to eat it." She went over and standing on her toes reached up and kissed him.

He put his arms around her waist, drawing her closer to him. "How the hell am I supposed to think about food when you're wearing this and half-naked?" He reached over and turned off the oven, picking her up and carrying her to the bedroom where he ravished her like a caveman who knew no boundaries. Two hours later they finally got out of bed and put some clothes on, though he would have loved for her to stay naked.

They ended up having a late supper, but neither one cared. They could have survived on sex alone, it filled them both. But that night they ended up going right to sleep, too tired to do anything else.

A few nights later they were laying on the sofa watching a movie when he got a call from Roy, saying he needed to talk to them and would be right over.

"What do you think he wants to talk to us about?" she asked, feeling as though her heart had jumped into her throat.

"I don't know, maybe he found out something about the site. He's good at his job and won't give up until these bastards are caught and put away. Then you'll be free and able to live a normal life."

"A normal life," she scoffed. "I haven't got a clue what that would be like," she said sadly.

His heart went out to her, she had a rough life right from the beginning. Once this mess was over with, he planned on helping her.

He loved her and started thinking about having a life with her someday. Pulling her into his arms he held her until they heard a knock at the door, knowing it had to be Roy he got up to answer it.

"Neil, sorry to pop in like this but I'd like to have a few words with Kiara."

"Sure, come on in, she's making coffee for us."
"Great, I could sure use one, it's been a long day," he said and went and sat on the chair across from the sofa.
She returned with coffee and biscuits for them.
"So what's up?" Neil asked, picking up his cup.
"I have started the investigation but I need some more information from Kiara. "Can you tell me anything about where they kept you and the other girls?"
"I'm afraid I can't be of much help. When I was put into the van they tied me up and put a blindfold over my eyes. My eyes were also covered when they took me from there and didn't take it off until we got here."
"What can you tell me about inside the house? Even the smallest detail, no matter how small and unimportant it might seem. Were you in a basement or another part of the house? Were there any smells or noises that might be out of the ordinary?"
"I remember the basement was cold and damp, there were several cells or cages. I saw at least a dozen women, we were all chained to the wall, some totally naked, some just in their bras and panties. The windows were painted with black paint and had bars on them. A door with locks on them was kept shut until one of the men came in to take one of the girls. I couldn't see what was on the other side."
"So what about when they brought you to Neil? They would have had to take you somewhere to clean you up. Tell me about that."

"Two men came and blindfolded me. I remember going up a flight of stairs and then I heard a loud noise, like another door opening. We went up another flight of stairs and I was taken down a hall into a room where they uncovered my eyes. There were two women there, really big and scary."

"Go on," Roy coached.

She looked at Neil and her eyes teared up, this next part was going to be embarrassing. "I could use something stronger," she said, putting her coffee down.

He squeezed her hand and got up, pouring scotch for him and Roy, giving her some wine.

"The two women stripped off my bra and panties and then they bathed me, and washed my hair. After the bath, I was tied naked to a table, my legs were forced open and they waxed me down there. I was then put into a dress, had make-up put on me and then they took a bunch of pictures." She started to cry when she remembered how rough they were, making crude remarks even though they were also women.

Neil pulled her into his arms, he didn't like seeing her in pain. "That's enough now," he snapped, looking at Roy.

"Neil, I need to know more about the house, any details."

"It's alright, I can go on," she said, wiping her tears when she looked at Neil. "It was an old house, one of those old Victorian homes, large. The drapes were closed so I couldn't see outside. I was put into one of the bedrooms on the upper level."

"Were you able to look out the window?" Roy asked, taking notes.

"No, they too were covered with black paint and had bars on them. I didn't hear any noise coming from outside. You know, like traffic, it was so quiet, almost as if we were in the country. The day they brought me here I was dressed up and given some clothes to take with me, they blindfolded me before we walked out of the house. I'm sorry, there's nothing else I can think of."

"You did good," Roy said, giving her a reassuring smile. "We have a couple of undercover agents working on the case. They are on the site and trying to get one of the girls. We're going to get them to talk, and maybe one of them will be able to give us more information. If only we knew where this house was." Can you describe the women, the ones who cleaned you up, and the person who took the pictures?"

"Yes," she answered, giving him a detailed description of everyone she saw in the house.

After writing down all of the information he stood up to leave. "I'll check into this, and see if we can come up with some names and an address. If you think of anything, call me. I'll get back to you both when I know more."

They walked Roy over to the door and just as he was walking she stopped him. "I remember something else. When we were in the van one of the men rolled down the window, maybe ten minutes after we left the house. Even though I couldn't see anything, I did smell something as we drove."

"What kind of smell?" Roy asked, taking out his notepad.

"Like fish."

Roy looked up from his notepad to look at her. "Maybe one of the men had fish for lunch or dinner."

She shakes her head. "No. I didn't smell it on them, not until the window was rolled down. It wasn't strong, but it was definitely fish."

"OK, that's good. I'll check out any factories or warehouses around. I'll be in touch," he said and walked out, bidding them goodnight.

Neil took her hand and walked over to the sofa and sat down, pulling her onto his lap. "I had no idea what you went through. I'm so sorry that happened to you. I wish I had the power to make it all go away."

"I didn't have it so bad, not like some of those other girls. They were beaten and raped, some were sold when they were no longer making money for them. Some didn't return, I think they were murdered. I didn't want to testify but now I do. Those women need to be saved and the bastards put away."

He touched her cheek with the palm of his hand. "I will be right by your side the whole time, holding your hand and keeping you

She looks at him, a single tear slid down her face. "I might not be alive today if it wasn't for you, you saved my life. I just hope I haven't put you in any danger."

"You haven't."
"These people are murderers and I'm afraid that if they find out that I'm here with you they'll kill you. Me, they will sell me or kill me too." She put her arms around his neck, resting her head against his.
"Let's go to bed," he said, knowing she was right but he also knew he wasn't going to let anything happen to either one of them.
"Neil, I have to tell you I only have two pills left."
"We'll have your prescription filled."
"The people who took me usually give them to us, if you had it filled they might know I'm with you and not Eric."
"I'll get Eric to call them and let them know he'll refill it for you. They probably won't mind as long as they don't have to pay. But I'm curious, why would they care if the girls are on the pill as they stated condoms have to be used at all times?"
"They don't want the women getting pregnant because that would mean they wouldn't be able to work and make money for them."
"Oh, yeah I get that. Let's get some sleep, I'll call Eric in the morning," he said, giving her a kiss as they went to sleep.

Chapter 9

Neil called Eric in the morning and told him to email the site, informing them he was having her prescription filled and that he would take care of the cost so they wouldn't have to worry about it. He wasn't surprised to hear that they phoned him, asking to talk with her but he had the smarts to tell them she was in the shower. He told them he was pleased with her performance and he didn't want them calling or coming around.

Later that day Eric showed up at Neil's hotel, and he made sure no one was following him. He went to his office, knocking before walking in. "I picked up that package you asked me to get," he said and sat down across from him.

"Thanks, I appreciate it," he said, taking the package from him and stuffing it into his pocket.

"So how's it going with you and Kiara?"

Neil told him about the visit from Roy. "I really hope he can get those pricks soon, she's starting to go stir crazy not getting out. I hate that we can't go out to dinner or dancing. I'm doing the best I can to keep her entertained, day time is the hardest for her as I'm down here working most of the day."

"Why don't you let me take her out to lunch."

He shook his head. "I don't think so." He didn't want her going anywhere without him, he wondered if he was being selfish in keeping her locked up inside his suite.

"Look, nothing is going to happen. If we're seen together by any of those guys it's alright, they'll be expecting it and it will give her a chance to get out of that room, even for a short time."

Neil sat back and scratched his chin, thinking. "I guess it wouldn't hurt as long as you stayed in the general area. Alright, I'll phone her and let her know you're coming up to take her out to lunch. Just be careful, make sure no one sees you leaving or coming back with her, take the back way and the stairs."

"I'll be careful."

"Alright, just let me call her first before you go up. I had told her not to open the door for anyone but if she knows you on your way up it'll be OK." He then made the call, after talking to her he hung up, turning to look at Eric. "You have to wait half an hour, she's going to shower first."

"I could help her with that," he said, smirking.

"Not funny," he said, giving Eric an angry glare and throwing a rolled-up piece of paper at him. He then took his wallet out and took out his credit card, handing it to him. "After lunch, you can take her shopping and tell her to buy whatever she wants."

Twenty minutes later Eric left to go pick up Kiara.

She greeted him with a smile. She was happy to be getting out, though she wished it was Neil she was going with. "Hi Eric, I'm ready to go, where are we going?"

"Since Neil would kill me if I took you too far away I thought I'd take you to this nice Italian place just down the road. He also told me to take you shopping and gave me his card to give you and said for you to buy whatever you want," he said, handing her the card.

She took it, and looking at it she shakes her head. "He has given me so much already."

"He loves you and would give you the world if he could. Now, let's head out, I'm starving." He explained to her why they were using the stairs and going out the back way.

They walked for about fifteen minutes before stopping at the restaurant where he opened the door for her to go in first. They were seated and handed a menu and asked if they would like a drink to start off with.

"I'll have a glass of white wine please, and for the lady," he said, looking at Kiara.

"I'll have the same."

After what she thought was the best lunch ever he took her for a walk down the strip, pointing out various shops.

"You know Neil wants you to buy something nice for yourself and yet at every clothing store we walked by you shook your head, not wanting to go in."

"I don't feel right spending his money and besides I haven't got a clue what to get."

Eric stopped, crossing his arms as he looked around. "This is just a suggestion but seeing that Valentine's day is coming up, why not get a sexy outfit to surprise Neil with? I can guarantee he'll love it. There's a store just down the road that specializes in such outfits, shall we go take a look?"

She thought about it, it would be nice to do something just for Neil as he had done so much for her so she nodded. "It wouldn't hurt to take a look."

Her face turned a light shade of red when they walked into the store and she saw all of the sexy and revealing outfits. There was also an assortment of sex toys, handcuffs, whips and so much more, she had no idea what most of them were for. She couldn't help giggling as she watched Eric, he was a kid in a candy store the way he was drooling as he checked out the sexy clothing.

"Oh man, I need to get me some of these," he said, picking up some handcuffs and whips.

"Do you guys really like this kind of stuff?" she asked curiously.

He smiled brightly at her and winked. "Hell yeah girl. There's nothing sexier than a beautiful woman handcuffed to your bed."

She wandered around the store until an outfit caught her eye. It was red, complete with stockings and a garter belt, it even had a red feather. She just knew Neil would love it but she felt shy about buying it with Eric there. She moved away when she saw him walking towards her carrying a small bag.

"I picked up a couple of things for myself, well, for the next lucky woman I meet," he said, holding up the bag. "Hey, aren't you going to get something?"

"I did see something but I'm not sure," she said, her face turning red.

He knew that look, signs of innocence and shyness when her face turned red. He got the feeling she wasn't going to buy anything with him standing around so he had an idea. "I'll tell you what, I'll go wait outside while you pick out what you want. Take your time, I'll be standing right out there," he said, pointing to the window.

She felt the anxiety sliding from her body when he said that. "OK, thank you. I'll try not to take too long." She waited until he was outside the store and went back to the outfit she had her eyes on. After searching for her size she then went and picked up a matching pair of furry handcuffs and a blindfold. The excitement was building up inside her, she could hardly wait for him to see her in it and to let him know she was willing to get kinky. It was going to be difficult waiting two days until Valentine's day and keeping it hidden so that he wouldn't see it until she had it on.

After paying for the items she had to wonder what the sales clerk was thinking. But seeing no emotion or expression on her face she figured the woman had seen it all. Picking up her bag she went outside where Eric was patiently waiting for her.

"So you're gonna show me what Eric asked, grinning at her. you bought it?"

"No way," she said, shaking her head.

He just laughed. "It was worth a shot. Let's stop for some ice cream before I take you back. I'll just call Neil to let him know what's taking so long. I bet he's been checking his watch ever since we left the hotel."

They stopped and went into the ice cream parlor and ordered a large banana split which they shared. He had her laughing, she felt grateful for him showing her a good time but said it was time she got back.

They walked back and went through the back way, again using the stairs.

He waited until she unlocked the door. "I really had a great time with you today but I should be on my way now."

"Did you want to come in for a coffee and wait for Neil? He should be back soon."

"I'd love to but I better not, he might not like it. I'll see you another time," he said and gave her a kiss on her cheek, and left.

Neil looked up when there was a knock and Eric walked in. He leaned back in his chair, glad that they were back, though they were gone longer than he expected. "So you finally decided to return."

Eric sat down. "We had a great afternoon, you're a very lucky man."

"I know," he answered. He took a small box out of his desk and opened it, showing off a pair of heart-shaped diamond earrings. I went and bought these for her, for Valentine's day. Do you think she'll like them?" He had spent over two hours in the jewelry store, looking for the right ones.

Eric picked them up and let out a whistle. "Holy shit man, these are gorgeous. Of course, she'll love them. You old softie, I've never known you to give any woman jewelry before."

"She's not just any woman, she's the one I'm going to marry."

Eric sat up straight, his eyes almost bulging out of his head. "Marry. I thought you said you would never get married."

"I did, didn't I? I meant it then, but now I know deep in my heart that we belong together. There was a force beyond our control that brought me to that kitten site and found her, it was meant to be." He looks at Eric. "You didn't try putting the moves on her right?"

"I flirted with her but she was immune to my charm, the girl only has eyes for you. Don't worry pal, I behaved like a perfect gentleman. You should finish up for the day, I think she is missing you."

Neil smiled. "I was just on my way up before you walked in. Thanks again for taking her out and showing her a good time. After what she's been through she deserves some fun."

Once Eric left she went and hid the clothes inside the closet, way in the back so that he wouldn't find them. Never would she have imagined dressing up in such clothing, but again she never thought she would do half the things she did with him. She changed into shorts and a tank top and went to start supper. Putting the meat into the oven she heard him coming in and went to greet him.

He smiled when he saw her, thinking she looked so cute and sexy in her shorts and her hair done up in a ponytail. He put his arms around her when she got to him, looking down at her. "I've missed you like crazy," he said, kissing her. It was such an amazing feeling coming home to a beautiful woman who greeted you with open arms and a hug. Taking a hold of her face he drew her up for a kiss, showing her just how much he missed her.

When they finally came up for air she moved from his embrace. "Dinner will be ready in an hour, let me go pour you a drink," she said, smiling as she walked over to the bar and poured him a glass of scotch.

He watched her as she walked away, enjoying the view of her long legs and her sweet ass which was just the right size and shape. He removed his tie and jacket before going to sit down and took the scotch from her, pulling her down next to him. “The day after tomorrow is Valentine's day and the hotel is booked solid so I'm going to be gone all day and won't be back until dinner time. I'm sorry I have to be gone so long but I will pop in and have a quick lunch with you."

She cuddled into him. This is your business, I understand but you won't have to go back out after dinner will you?"

"No baby, I'm all yours that night.”

“Good,” she said, jumping off his lap to go check on the meal.

It was Valentine's day and when she woke up he had already left for work, but there was a single red rose laying on his pillow. Reaching to sit over she picks it up and smiles, holding it to her nose. Getting up she throws on a robe and goes to the kitchen to make some coffee. There, on the table were a dozen red roses in a glass vase and a card next to them. They were the same as the ones he had left on the pillow. Picking up the card she felt the tears coming when she read the note from him.

Happy Valentine's Day sweetheart. Since you have come into my life the sun shines brighter, the air is fresher and the food tastes better. My heart is now filled with happiness and love. I never knew life could be this amazing before, you showed me how to love and to know what it's like to be loved. I love you with all of my heart. Love Neil.

Pouring a cup of coffee she sat down, pulling the vase closer to smell the flowers, she loved the smell of roses. This was the first time she had ever gotten flowers from anyone, it made her feel special. Now she was glad she had bought the sexy outfit and she was going to give him the best Valentine's day ever.

She would make him a nice lunch and then when he came back after he was done work for the day she would be in the clothes she bought, surprising him. But she was a little nervous about being handcuffed and blindfolded but was willing to do anything to make the man she loved happy.

Checking his watch and seeing it was lunchtime he hurried up to his suite, he had promised to have lunch with her. As soon as he walked in she jumped into his arms, showering his face with kisses.

"Thank you for the flowers, I love them," she said, pulling him into the kitchen.

He sat down and they ate. “I really wish I could stay longer but I have to get back as soon as I'm done eating."

"I know, I'm just glad you're here now."

When they were done she walked him to the door where he pulled her into his arms, giving her a long and passionate kiss. "Happy Valentine's day baby, I'll be back by seven." Giving her another kiss he left to go back downstairs.

It was the busiest day of the year, all the rooms were booked, the dining room filled and the casino was buzzing with people and slot machines dinging. It was ten minutes to seven so taking the earrings out of the desk drawer he placed them in his jacket. Knowing he was on his way to see Kiara he was in a great mood so he instructed his staff to give everyone a free glass of their best champagne.

He entered the suite and closed the door. "Babe, I'm home."

"Come into the bedroom," she calls out to him.

As he walks towards the bedroom he loosens his tie, he stopped in the doorway, his eyes wide and his jaw dropped.

"Holy shit," he said quietly under his breath. He took her all in, staring at her face, moving down, and stopping to admire her breasts that were pushed up. He then traveled down to her legs with the red fishnet stockings. He swiftly removed his jacket, tie, and shirt, tossing them to the floor.

"Happy Valentine's day," she said and started dancing provocatively.

His heart was pounding, his cock hard as he watched her place her leg around the bedpost and grind against it. Tossing her head back she swayed her ass back and forth. Then looking at him she licked her lips. He couldn't take it another minute, he rushed over and was about to take her in his arms when she pushed him down onto the bed.

She straddled him, pinning his hands above his head. "Do you like the outfit? I picked it out just for you."

"Oh yeah, I like it a lot." He saw her pick up the handcuffs. "What are you planning on doing with those?" He was taken by complete surprise by how fast she was cuffing his hands to the bedpost. "Babe, take them off me."

Smiling, she put the red blindfold over his eyes. "You know what I'm doing with them, now be a good boy and just relax. This is my gift to you, enjoy."

Neil was never the one tied up and blindfolded before and he did find it to be arousing. He felt his member growing and throbbing inside his pants when her lips went to his neck and started kissing, moving down. He felt her tongue on his chest, moving down, she unbuckled his belt and pulled his pants and briefs off. He let out a moan when she started licking and sucking on the tip of his shaft before taking him all in. This time she did not gag but continued tickling him with her tongue, her fingers massaging his balls. He tried reaching down to grab her, forgetting she had him cuffed.

"Did you like that baby," she asked, straddling him as she wiped her mouth. She really didn't have to ask him, she could tell by the way he moaned and how his body reacted when he came hard and fast.

"I think you already know the answer to that, now untie me."

She takes off his blindfold and picks up the feather. "Maybe I'm not done with you yet." She leaned down and kissed him, she liked that he was completely at her mercy. She then laid on him, her kiss hot and demanding, pushing her tongue inside his mouth, she felt him getting hard again.

"Kiara, untie me, it's your turn." Damn, he was hard again and wanted to be inside her sweetness, but first, it was her turn to be pleased.

She nodded, her panties were wet and her core was throbbing, she wanted him badly. Removing the cuffs she squealed when he grabbed her so fast, flipping her onto her back and covering her body with his.

He gave her a wicked grin as he cuffed her to the bed. "I love what you're wearing, it really turned me on so now I'm going to have some real fun with you." He then put the blindfold over her eyes.

He lowered his mouth onto hers, and his one hand moved down to between her legs and inside her panties, he started rubbing her pussy, she was so wet and she started squirming, her purr-like moans got him even harder than he already was. His lips moved down to the top of her breasts, wanting to feel them in his mouth but the damn material was in the way. It was time he stripped her down naked.

He started by unclipping the stockings from the garter belt and slowly pulled each one off. Kissing her legs as he moved up, leaving her panties for last. He heard her giggling when he had trouble unclipping the buttons on the body garment and swearing. “You think this is funny?" he asked, anxious to get her naked.

"A little," she answered. Then she felt the tearing of her clothes as he ripped them and tore them off her. "Neil, this was very expensive."

"Oh well, they shouldn't make it so hard to undo. Now no more talking or I'll have to punish you, just lay back and enjoy."

She had no choice but to lay there as she was cuffed to the bed, she could hear the sound of his pants dropping to the floor. Then her body was covered in goosebumps when he moved the feather over her neck. He moved it down to her breasts, using it to tickle the nipples, getting them hard. She began breathing heavily, her body starting to twitch when the feather went down her legs and he opened her legs, using it to tickle her pussy. "Oh Neil, she moaned when he dropped it and his head replaced the feather and his tongue took over. He sucked on her clit, drawing it between his lips. She arched her back when his tongue flicked in and out of her like a lizard's tongue catching its prey. She couldn't hold back when her orgasm hit her like a ton of bricks. "Yes, oh my God yes," she cried out, the trembling stopped and she relaxed. "That was amazing but I can't take it anymore, I'm exhausted."

He moved up to her, laying on top of her. "Oh sweetheart, I'm nowhere done with you." He kissed her hard, pressing her head back into the pillow, his hand caressing her breasts. As much as he hated leaving the softness of her lips he was dying to taste her breasts in his mouth. His cock was hard, pressing against her as he sucked and licked each breast until she let out some small panting moans. He placed his hand over her neck, the other one caressing her breasts as he kept sliding his shaft over her wet opening. He got a great deal of pleasure when she begged him to take her as she lifted her hips up, letting him know she wanted him inside her.

She couldn't see a thing, but what he was doing to her, the way she was feeling was driving her mad with desire. She wanted him so bad that the throbbing deep inside of her core was starting to hurt. "Please, I'm on fire, you need to put it out."

He stopped sucking on her neck to look down at her. "What is it you want me to do?"

"You know what I want," she said, yanking on the cuffs in frustration.

"Tell me what you want and talk dirty or I'll keep on teasing you," he said, grinning, knowing she couldn't see him.

"I want you to fuck me," she said almost shyly.

He placed two fingers inside her. Is this what you want?"

Her head rolled from side to side, he was quickly bringing her to another orgasm even though she wanted him inside of her. "Untie me," she said when her heart stopped racing after another orgasm, she was exhausted.

He felt he had enough of teasing her so he untied her, took off the blindfold, and spread her legs he slowly entered her. His lips came down hard on hers as he kissed her with a deep passion that rocked them both. He was ready for his own release when he felt her warmth wrapped around his manhood, he started moving up and down faster and faster until he could not hold back, his balls tight and aching he gave a few more hard thrusts into her, they both came like a volcano erupting. He collapsed on top of her, burying his face in the crook of her neck, feeling her legs wrapping around his waist and her arms around his neck.

He lifted himself up, looking down at her as she moved his hair from his face. "I love you," he said, kissing her before rolling off her.

"Happy Valentine's day," she said, looking at him as she pulled the sheet over her breasts that were still rising and falling rapidly.

"That reminds me," he said and jumping out of bed went over to where he had thrown his jacket and took out the small black velvet box that had a tiny red bow on top. Getting back into bed he holds it out towards her. "Happy Valentine's day sweetheart."

She looks at it and then at him, not believing her eyes. "You bought me something?"

"Well yeah, it's a special day, here, open it."

Opening it she saw the heart-shaped diamond earrings and gasped, covering her mouth with one hand while the other one held the box. "Oh my God, these are so beautiful, look at how they sparkle."

"I'm glad you like them."

"I love them," she said and she couldn't hold back the tears that fell from her eyes.

"If you love them, then why are you crying?" he asked, wiping her tears away.

"No one has given me anything this beautiful before, actually this is the very first gift I've ever gotten."

"Surely you have gotten gifts on your birthday or Christmas."

"No, never."

He felt so bad for her and made up his mind that once this mess was behind them he would shower her with tons of gifts on her birthdays and other occasions.

Smiling, she takes the earrings out of the box and puts them on, facing him. "How do they look?"

"They're nice, but it's you that makes them look beautiful," he said, drawing her closer to kiss her.

Chapter 10

When he woke up the next morning he turned his head to look at her. He had to smile when he saw she was still wearing the earrings. He'll never get over the look in her eyes when she opens the box, her eyes lighting up. She was curled up into a ball as she lay next to him. He reached over to touch her lips, they looked pouty when she slept.

Opening her eyes she giggled. "What are you doing?" she asked, feeling his fingers in her mouth.

"I love your lips and I was hoping you would wake up so I could kiss them."

"I'm awake."

Putting one leg over her he climbs on top of her, using his hands to hold him up. "Last night was amazing. I hope you surprise me like that again in the future," he said before lowering his head to kiss her. That kiss led to more as his hand traveled down the side of her body until he reached between her legs. The way she moved her lips against his and her legs brushing against his got him so turned on, he entered her, making her squirm madly beneath him. Later, they showered and dressed, making breakfast together.

After he left to do some work she cleaned the suite, with the radio playing she danced around like a teenager in love. Growing up and seeing how badly the men treated her mother she thought that was how it was in a relationship. But Neil showed her how wrong she was, he was gentle, and loving and never laid a hand on her in violence. She had supper made for him when he came back and had missed him all day she ran into his arms. It made her feel so special when he lifted her up off her feet and kissed her.

It melted his heart to see the way she looked at him whenever he entered a room. There was so much love in her eyes, she made him feel like a hero. He prayed that he would be able to live up to her expectations. He loved the way she melted in his arms, her lips so soft against his. "Wow, I could really get used to this kind of welcoming every time I come home," he said, breaking the kiss to touch her cheek.

"Get used to it," she answered, walking away and pouring him a shot of scotch. "Sit down and relax while I finish dinner," she said, handing him his drink.

Taking off his jacket and tie he went and sat down, looking around the room, it was spotless. She kept the place so clean and he was starting to feel guilty. He didn't want her to think she had to do this to please him and wondered if she was bored with nothing else to do. Later he would have a talk with her to see if she had any hobbies or interests.

"Dinner's ready," she shouted out from the kitchen. She dished out their food and placed the plates on the table. "I hope you like lasagna."

"I love it," he answered, taking a bite of it. "Wow, this is really good. Kiara, I love that you cook and clean but I don't want you to think you have to do it. Isn't there something else you'd like to do?"

"I don't mind, it keeps me busy."

"Don't you have any hobbies or something you'd rather be doing?"

"Growing up I never had time for hobbies, it was all I could manage to finish high school. I practically raised myself. I cooked and cleaned for my mother and me."

"Did you have any favorite subjects in school?"

"I liked the business classes, learning how to type, do books, and the rest of it. I even had dreams of going to college and getting a business degree."

"It's not too late, you could take some classes and do most of them on the internet. I could help get you set up. After we eat we'll go online and see what we have to do to get you registered. Getting your business degree online might take longer but it'll be worth it."

"You really think I could do that?"

"People do it all the time and yes, I not only think you can do it, I know you can." It did his heart good to see her face light up and excited about something.

After they ate and the dishes were done they sat on the sofa, her between his legs as they searched the internet for classes and to register.

Two hours later he helped her fill out the forms and had to argue with her about him paying for them. He had his finger on the button to send, he looked at her before pushing it. "Are you sure this is what you want?"

She sucked her bottom lip under her top teeth and nodded.

"OK then, here we go," he said, then he pushed send.

"I will pay you back."

"Kiara, don't worry about it, it's my gift to you."

She shifted her body so that she was straddling him, putting her hands on his chest. "You've done so much for me already."

"I love you, there's nothing I wouldn't do for you." He flipped her over so that she was laying on her back and he was on top of her. "There is something you can do for me," he said, lowering his head and kissing her, and just when things were getting hot and heavy there was a knock at the door.

"You better get that, it might be important," she said as he kept kissing her neck and his hand went down her panties. She could feel how excited he was as his manhood was pressing against her.

"Shit," he swore and got up, adjusting his crotch. "This better be important," he said as he went over and opened the door with a scowl on his face.

"I hope I'm not interrupting anything?" Roy said with a smirk on his face as he entered the room. He could tell by Neil's flushed face that he was getting busy with Kiara. She confirmed it when he saw her buttoning up her blouse.

"As a matter of fact, you are. You could have phoned to let me know you were coming."

"I did, several times but you didn't answer your phone."

"I must have turned off my phone. Well since you're here you might as well sit down and tell us what you want."

Roy walked over to her, giving her a hug. "I'm sorry to disturb you but I have a few more questions to ask you and I also have some pictures for you to look at." He sat down and waited for Neil to join them.

Neil poured them all a drink and sat down next to her.

Roy opened a large brown envelope and took out the pictures. “Do you recognize any of these people?"

Her hands began to shake. "This was one of the women who cleaned me up," she said, handing him back the one picture of a stout woman in her late forties. "This was the other one and these two men were the ones that brought me here," she said, handing Roy those ones too.

"What about these girls?" Roy asked, handing her some more pictures.

She looked at four girls and handed him one back. "This girl, she was in the cage next to mine. My god, she was much younger than me, maybe sixteen. But here with all the makeup and what she's wearing she could pass for twenty."

"Where did you get these pictures from?" Neil asked as he too looked at them.

"For the past week, we've been searching the area around a fresh seafood processing factory within the time frame Kiara said the drive took from where she was to here." He looks at her. "It's a good thing that man rolled down his window and you remembered the smell. I honestly didn't know there was a factory out there. We searched the woods and there was a house, more like an old mansion that was a bit run down."

"So you have the bastards, why aren't they in custody?" Neil snapped, feeling frustrated.

"It's not that simple. We have the place under watch but there's nothing suspicious going on that we can see. But now that Kiara has identified this girl we can now go ahead and get a search warrant to go in. It will take a couple of days to get it so hang tight."

Neil took her hand and held it. "So once you go in and find the room where they are keeping the women you'll be able to put them behind bars and she'll be safe, right?"

"If all goes well yes." He turned back to her. "I have one more picture to show you, have you ever seen this man before?" He hands her the picture of a man in his early thirties, tall with dark hair, and judging from the way he was dressed it looked like he was wealthy.

"Oh my God," she gasped, her face turned pale and her body trembled. "That's Charlie."

Neil turned his head sharply towards her. "Charlie, as in your ex?"

She looks at him and nods. "Yes, Charlie Richards." She looks at Roy. "I was living on the streets and he helped me, took me in and we became a couple. Until he kicked me out when I refused to have a threesome. What has he got to do with all of this?"

"I'm not sure yet but he was seen going inside that house and coming out an hour later. We've been keeping an eye on him but when we checked into his background we didn't come up with much. Can you tell me what he does for a living?"

"All he ever told me was that he was a traveling salesman and he was gone a lot, sometimes for two days at a time."

"He has quite a fancy place for being a salesman and he drives a Porsche."

"I never questioned him about his job. I was just so grateful that he took me in and thought he really cared about me. At first, he was so nice and treated me well. I was young and naive, I wasn't aware of the dangers of living on the streets or how I could be taken and put into sex slavery."

"I thought you had some guys trying to hire a girl from the kitten site?" Neil asked.

"They tried, but so far haven't been accepted."

Neil shook his head, he was hoping that plan would have gotten them somewhere.

Roy rubbed his temple. "Hundreds of young girls go missing from around the world. Most of them are runaways who for whatever reason end up on the street. They are easily taken advantage of by men who promise them a better life. They clothe and feed them, shelter them and once they gain their trust the bastards put them into the sex trade. Young and scared they are forced to do it. But with your help, we can at least shut this ring down."

"So now what?" Neil asked.

"As soon as we get the search warrant we'll go in and search the house from top to bottom. If the girls are there we'll get them out and arrest the bastards.

In the meantime, we'll keep an eye on the place. I'll also be checking out this Charlie guy, I'll bring him in for questioning. For now, just lay low."

They stood when he did. "Keep us posted," he said and walked Roy to the door.

She went and stood by the window, looking out. She felt his arms going around her waist and she leaned her head back against his chest. "I'm scared," she said, shedding some tears.

"You're safe with me."

She turned around to face him. "Charlie must be a part of this and to think I gave my virginity to that man. I feel so used and dirty. How can you bear to touch me?"

He cupped her face in his hands. “You were one of his victims, probably one of many. I love you, nothing you did or didn't do could stop me from wanting or loving you." He wrapped his arms around her, wanting to keep her safe.

"I remember this one girl I met when I was living on the streets. She ran away from home because she didn't like the rules her parents set out. She couldn't have been more than sixteen and she started turning tricks to make enough for food. Then one day she disappeared, and I never saw her again. Why can't these girls understand that their parents set rules to protect them? It was different for me, my mother died and I couldn't pay the rent. But I never turned tricks and yet I was taken and made to be a sex kitten."

"I know the baby and I thank God every morning that he sent you to me first. If Roy can get those girls out then that's a few that will be saved, maybe they will find their way back home."

"I'm so exhausted, this is getting too much to handle," she said and broke down crying, letting him comfort her.

He picked her up and carried her to the bed where they got undressed and laid down. He didn't do anything but hold her, stroking her back and trying to reassure her that everything would be alright."

Neil woke up first and saw her laying on her side, he had stayed awake worrying about her and made a decision. So leaning over her he starts kissing the side of her face. It didn't take much to wake her up and when she did she smiled.

"Morning," she purred softly.

"Hey beautiful, I've got a surprise for you."

"Neil, it's not a surprise, I can feel it poking me," she answered, giggling. She turned over onto her back and put her arms around his neck.

When she lifted her hips to rub against him he forgot about what he wanted to tell her, instead he kissed her passionately. Soon they were caressing and groping each other, their desire grew and they made love.

An hour later he rolled off her and onto his side, pulling her in close to him. "I'm taking you away for a few days."

She tilted her head up to look at him. "Why, where?"

"I think you need to get away from here, to be able to go out in public and have some fun. I'm not sure yet. I need to clear my schedule and make sure things are on track here before we leave. We will leave on Friday."

"Are you only doing this to get me away when Roy and his men raid the house?"

"That's part of it, but I also think it'll do you good to get away. Roy actually suggested it a while back. I also want to be able to take you out to dinner and maybe some dancing. But it depends on where we go." He had it all planned out in his head, they would sneak away late Friday night and just drive until he figured they were far enough away.

The night before they were going to leave Eric showed up at Neil's place with two large pizzas and a couple of bottles of wine. "Hey guys, I was thinking you might be getting bored up here by yourselves so I thought I would come to keep you company."

Neil would have preferred to be alone with Kiara but seeing that Eric was his friend and helped him out he welcomed him in. "Pizza sounds great, come on in," he said, grabbing the wine from him.

"Where's Kiara?" he asked, setting the food down on the coffee table.

"She's taking a shower but she'll be out soon. Open the wine while I go and let her know you're here."

"Just don't decide to join her and leave me here all alone," he said, chuckling.

Neil shook his head as he walked away and headed into the bedroom. She was just stepping out of the shower and he handed her a towel, getting a good look first.

"You could have joined me or if you want I'll go back in with you," she said, giving him a sexy smile.

He smiled back, he liked that idea. "As hot as that sounds I'm afraid we can't, we have company. Eric is here and he brought pizza. I wanted to warn you so that you didn't come out with something revealing." He pulled her into his arms and kissed her before pulling away. "I'll see you after you put some clothes on."

The men were talking and joking around when she came into the room wearing jeans and a cotton blouse. Seeing the pizza her stomach growled, she loved pizza, it was her favorite thing to eat. When the guys stood up she felt a sense of worth overcome her. No one had ever treated her with such respect before and these two guys made her feel good about herself.

"Get some while it's hot," Eric said and handed her a plate and poured her some wine.

They talked, ate, and then decided to play a board game.

"I'm taking Kiara away for a few days," Neil said as he rolled the dice.

Eric's eyes shot up to look at him. “Do you think that's wise? What if someone sees you together, isn't it safer for her to stay here?"

"We're going far enough away where no one knows us and it's only for a short time. I need to get away from here, the last few days have been crazy downstairs."

"Where are you going to go?"

"Nowhere in particular. I'm just going to keep driving until I find a place where we can be alone and relax." He looked up at Eric. "It sounds to me like you have a problem with us going away."

Eric shook his head. "No, I don't have a problem, I think it will do you both a world of good to get out of here. I'm just worried about the two of you out there alone with no backup. At least here you have the safety of your home and your brother-in-law to help protect you both."

"OK you guys, enough serious talk, are we playing this game or what?" she asked, hiccupping loudly. "Oh, excuse me," she said, covering her mouth when she hiccupped again.

Both men looked at each other and smiled. Her cheeks were getting red and she was slurring her words, they knew she was getting wasted. When she went to stand up she staggered backward, landing in Neil's lap and she giggled, followed by another hiccup.

She put her arms around his neck. "I think I've had too much to drink, maybe you should put me to bed."

He lifted her up into his arms. "Just give me a minute and I'll be right back," he said to Eric as he carried her to the bedroom.

"Night Eric," she said, waving to him as she was carried away.

He laid her down on the bed and helped her get undressed, not bothering to put her nightgown on, he just covered her up with the covers. He preferred it when she slept naked, he loved the feel of her warm naked skin against his.

When he went to kiss her she put her hands around his neck. "Come to bed and I'll do things to you that will make you scream out my name," she said, yawning.

He let out a chuckle. "Sounds good but you're in no shape to do anything. Get some sleep baby and I'll be with you shortly." He gave her a tender kiss before she fell asleep. He was so much in love with her, and not just her body but all of her. He took one last look at her sleeping before going back to join Eric.

"Someone is going to feel like crap when they wake up," Eric said, smirking.

"She was out like a light the moment her head hit the pillow. Damn it, Eric, I never knew love could feel so good and I owe it all to you."

"Me, what did I do?"

"It was you who spotted her profile and pointed her out. You helped me to find the love of my life and for that, I will forever be grateful to you."

"I'm glad I could help. She is special and obviously didn't belong on that site. I'm actually jealous of you and wished I had gone on there and found her for myself. Who knows, we might have hit it off and she could have been the love of my life."

"Eric, it doesn't work that way. Kiara and I had this instant connection, there was chemistry and sparks between us right from the moment she first walked in my door. Don't worry buddy, there's a special woman out there for you."

"Yeah, maybe. So have you heard any more from Roy on the case, has he got any leads?"
"They found what they believe is the house where the girls are kept. It's been under surveillance for a few days and they spotted the two men who brought Kiara here going in and out. They are waiting for the warrant to search the place, which should be any time now."
"Wow, how did they know where to look?"
"She remembered a smell when they were bringing her here, a fishy smell so the cops searched and found a factory that processed seafood. I guess the house was hidden in the woods, out of view."
"She's a clever girl," Eric said, scratching the back of his head.
"You want to know what else?"
"Sure," he answered, all ears.
"Her ex, Charlie Richards was seen going in and leaving an hour later."
"So you think he is in on it?"
"It appears so, but what his involvement is we aren't sure and won't know until he's taken in for questioning."
"Have they not done that yet?"
"I guess not since I haven't heard back from Roy. It's only a matter of time before they get those guys and shut them down. Once that happens Kiara can move on with her life, and we both can. Until then I'll make sure she's safe and those pricks don't get their hands on her."

"They better hurry, she's only got two and a half weeks left before I have to hand her back over to the site. What are you going to do if it's not been resolved by then?"

"Then I'll take her away from here. Roy was saying he could put her into the witness protection program. If it comes to that then I'll be going with her."

"I was just thinking, maybe you should let me take her away instead of you. It might be safer for all of us and you have your business to take care of. You know she'll be safe with me and I won't make any moves on her."

"I appreciate the offer but I doubt she'll go anywhere without me. Besides, I want this time away with her and I can keep her safe."

Eric just sat and stared at him for a moment, he knew he wasn't going to change Neil's mind about him taking her so he dropped the subject. "OK, just be careful and watch your back. It's getting late so I'll be on my way. Have a safe trip and I'll see you when you get back."

He walked Eric over to the door, he promised to call him once he got back from their trip. He was getting the feeling that Eric had a tiny crush on Keira but he also trusted Eric and knew he would never try anything with her. After tidying up the mess he went to bed, taking off his clothes he got in next to her, putting his arm around her. She didn't wake up when he pulled her closer, only snuggled into him.

He woke up early to the sound of her puking in the bathroom, getting up he grabbed her robe and went to see if she was alright. She was on her knees with her head over the bowl so he went over, placing her robe over her shoulders, and then holding her hair back.

"Oh God, why did I have to drink so much," she said, her throat so dry and scratchy.

"I shouldn't have let you but you were having so much fun," he said, placing a kiss on her neck. When she was done he helped her up. "You go back to bed and get some rest."

"But on our trip, I need to pack and get ready."

"We're not leaving until late tonight so there's plenty of time, now back to bed."

"Alright, just let me wash up and brush my teeth."

While she was doing that he went and made her some tea and dry toast, he found her in bed, she had put on a nightgown by the time he returned to the bedroom. "I hear dry toast is good for an upset stomach."

"Thank you," she said, taking a sip of her tea. "I hope I didn't make a fool of myself last night around Eric."

"You didn't, you were funny. I have some things to do downstairs so while I'm gone I want you to get plenty of rest. You can pack later when you're feeling better. Oh, and make sure to bring along a nice dress, I plan on taking you to dinner and dancing at some point."

Her eyes lit up when she smiled. "Oh I can't wait, I'll finally get to wear the earrings you bought me."

"You have been wearing them."
"I know, around here but I want to be able to wear them with a nice dress outside the suite."
He placed the palm of his hand against the side of her face. "I know sweetheart and when this mess with the site is over with I'll take you out all the time, to wherever you want to go. I love you, now I really have to get going." He pulled her close, giving her a long and loving kiss before leaving.

Chapter 11

They were all packed and ready to leave by midnight, going out the back way and down the stairs to the underground parking. After the bags were put in the trunk he opened her door for her and waited until she was seated before going around to the driver's side. She was excited about going away with him and was curious as to where they would end up. During the drive, she told him more about herself and he also told her about himself. After a little over four hours of driving, they ended up in Santa Ana, Ca.

"This looks like a good place to stay for a few days," he said when he pulled up to a hotel and parked in the parking lot.

"Don't we need a reservation to stay here? It looks kind of fancy," she asked, looking up at the hotel.

"Usually you have to but since it's not their busy season we shouldn't have a problem getting a room." He gets out and going around opens her door then takes the bags from his trunk.

They were in luck, there were plenty of rooms, and had no problems getting one of their finest suites.

She took a look around and sat on the bed, smiling at him. "The room is beautiful, but we could have stayed at one of the least expensive ones. I can't wait to go exploring and see the sights, I hear they have some cool museums."

"Tomorrow baby, but right now I want to rip off your clothes and do some really naughty things to you." Taking off his shirt he moved closer and laid her back down on the bed.

Her hands went onto his head and she drew him in for a kiss. She loved the feel of his strong arms on her, the way it felt when his shaft got hard and pressed against her. Her nipples grew hard, her core hot and throbbing and she felt her panties getting damp. He had this power over her, one that could get the fire inside her rising. She undid his pants when he pulled off her dress and threw it onto the floor. Her hands moved over his muscular back when he spread her legs open and entered her swiftly, making her gasp. For over an hour he licked and sucked every inch of her, making her beg him to stop teasing her. He finally gave in, giving her what she wanted, what they both wanted.

Morning: Neil let out a grunt when he felt her weight on top of him, she was bouncing and rubbing his chest, trying to wake him.

"Neil, wake up, it's morning and I want to go out sightseeing."

He opened his eyes, feeling his manhood growing. "If you keep jumping on me like this the only thing you're going to see is the ceiling."

Realizing the effect she was having on him she jumped off him and out of the bed. "I've already had my shower and made you coffee," she said, picking it up and handing it to him. "Drink this and go shower."

Taking a look at her over the rim of the mug he takes a sip. “You're awfully bossy."

She smiled back at him. "I just want to enjoy the time here."

"Shower with me," he said, placing his mug down. He got out of bed and walked over to her without a stitch of clothing on.

"I already showered and I know you way too well. If I went in there with you we wouldn't be leaving this room until noon. Please, get ready and take me out, please," she said, running her hands over his chest and giving him puppy eyes.

"You and those beautiful green eyes of yours, and when you give me that look I can't refuse you anything," he said when he cupped her chin in his hand. Pulling her closer he kissed her before heading into the shower.

He took her out for breakfast first then they walked down the street, stopping at one of the museums and looking around. After that, they took a boat tour and stopped to buy fresh fruit at one of the many outdoor markets. They dined that night in the hotel dining room, ordering lobster and salad.

For the next two days, they went sightseeing, shopping, and ate at some of the finest restaurants around. They went swimming and at night had amazing, mind-blowing sex.

On the fourth night, he took her to a nightclub that had a live band playing. She wore a short black dress and her diamond earrings, he thought she was the prettiest woman in the whole place. So did all the other men who stared at her when they walked by. He found them a table on the higher level by the side where they could look down at the people dancing. She asked for a beer and he ordered one for both of them. She was annoyed when the female server made a point of rubbing up against him when she placed the drinks down. But she kept quiet, not wanting to cause a scene.

"This is nice," she said loudly so he could hear her over the music. "Let's dance."

He looked down and when he saw the way they were dancing, their bodies grinding against each other and jumping all around he shook his head. "I can't dance to that garbage. Let's wait until they play something slower."

She wasn't about to let him get away with it, she wanted to dance so standing up she took his hands and pulled him up. "Come on, just try it for me."

"I don't know how to dance to this."

"You don't have to know how. Just move your body and arms around," she said, dragging him down the steps and over to the dance floor.

"I feel foolish," he said as he tried moving his body the way the others were doing.

"You're doing great," she yelled back at him, swaying her hips and bumping into his. She could tell he was uncomfortable but loved the fact that he was trying to do it for her.

Neil looked around, he really hated this and then when a slow song came on he let out a deep breath and pulled her into his arms. "Now this is more my speed," he said, putting his arms around her. "Are you having fun, sweetheart?"

"Oh yes, are you?"

"I always do when I'm with you," he said, leaning over as he kissed her. After two slow songs the fast ones started up again, and he took hold of her hand. "I really don't want to dance to this, it's just not me."

"Then let's sit down and have a drink," she said, leading him off the dance floor and back to their table.

He reached over to take her hand. "I'm not much fun am I? If you want to dance with someone I won't get mad." Even saying this he knew he was lying, it would drive him mad seeing her with another man.

"You are fun and I don't want to dance with anyone but you. I do need to use the lady's room so will you excuse me?" She got up, gave him a kiss, and went to where the sign pointed to the washrooms. When she came back out she saw the female server at their table, she was looking at Neil as if she wanted to fuck him right there. Then the woman slipped him a piece of paper and walked away. She felt as if her head was going to explode, her blood was at the boiling point.

She sat down, looked at the piece of paper that was crumpled up, and tossed it to the side. "What's that?" she asked, pointing to it.

"It's nothing," he answered.

"It doesn't look like anything to me. I saw that tramp handing it to you, is it her phone number?" Not waiting for him to answer, she picked it up and read it. “It's her phone number."

"Yes, but I told her I wasn't interested as you can clearly see."

"She has some nerve." Getting up she heads towards the bar where the woman was talking to another male customer.

Neil saw the anger in her eyes and knew there was going to be trouble, tossing some money down on the table he followed her. He got to her just as she reached the woman and he put his hand on her arm. "Kiara just leaves it, and let's go."

She shrugged him off, tapped the woman on her shoulder, and when she turned around she let her have it. “Look here bitch, let me give you a tip. Stop giving your number out to men who are with someone else."

The woman looked at her and smirked. "I didn't see a ring on his finger, BITCH.”

"He's mine," She hissed and tearing up the piece of paper into tiny pieces threw them in the woman's face. "Keep your hands off him."

Eyes were starting to turn when they heard the commotion so he grabbed her arm before Kiara could throw the first punch.

She struggled, looking back to glare at the woman when Neil dragged her out of the club. When they got outside into the cool night air she was able to calm down, then started feeling foolish. “Oh Neil, I'm so sorry."

"What are you sorry about?"

"For the horrible way I behaved there, it wasn't very ladylike. I wouldn't blame you if you were mad at me."

Putting his hands on her shoulders he smiled. "I'm not mad. I kind of like this jealous side of you, it's a bit of a turn-on."

Rolling her eyes she turned her head. "Only you could get turned on by that. Yes, I admit I was jealous. That bitch made a point of touching you every time she came to our table. Do you like it when women shamefully flirt with you?"

"I don't even notice anymore."

She looked back at him and smiled. "You really think you're all that, God's gift to women?"

He pulled her into his arms, his mouth so close to hers he could smell the wine on her breath. "I only want you, no one else. I'm going to kiss you now," he said as his lips landed on hers. His arms tightened around her, crushing her lips beneath his. When he broke the kiss and looked at her she had her eyes closed, lips still parted. "Would you like to go to another club or back to the hotel?"

Her eyes opened, her breath hitching in her throat when she spoke. "Hotel," she said, barely getting the words out.

As soon as they entered their hotel room he grabbed her, putting her up against the wall, pinning her hands above her head with his one hand. The other hand went up under her dress and inside her panties while he sucked on her neck. The more she moaned the more he stroked inside her, feeling how wet and hot she was. He felt her fingers going through his hair, yanking as she reached her climax.

Lips locked they started removing each other's clothes, he pulled her panties down and she kicked them away. Both naked, his shaft pressing against her he lifted her up as she wrapped her legs around his waist when he entered her. Her hands hung onto his shoulders when he started thrusting hard inside her, making her grunt as he kept pounding, her back hitting the wall with each thrust.

Sweating like a pig he rested his head against hers, his hands still under her firm butt as he held her up. "Christ, you're going to be the death of my one-eyed willie."

She started giggling. "I've never heard it called that before."

He pulled out and set her down on her feet, he was getting hard again and ready for another round. Taking her hand led her over to a chair and sitting down had her straddle him. "Time to put the snake back into your cave."

After two more days of relaxing and hot sex, it was time to go back home. Neil was anxious to find out if Roy had gotten anywhere on the case, he wanted this to be over with as soon as possible.

It was late when they got back home to Las Vegas, both tired from the drive they went right to sleep. He would wait until morning to call Roy and let him know they were home. But he was dying to know what all took place while they were gone, he hoped it was all over with and the bastards were caught.

He was awakened early by the ringing of his phone. Checking to make sure she was still asleep he gets out of bed and answers his phone he steps into the other room. It was Roy who said he'd be over to talk to him within the hour. He went and started the coffee before going to put some clothes on. After all, he couldn't greet his brother-in-law stark naked.

She woke up just as he walked into the bedroom and when she saw him picking up his pants she stopped him. "Come to bed," she said in a deep sexy tone.

"Roy's on his way over so I have to get dressed."

Tossing the covers off and letting him see her nakedness she pouted. "He's not here yet."

Dropping his pants he goes over and climbs on top of her. "Damn, you are so irresistible. I suppose we have time as long as we make it a quick one."

Just as things were getting hot and heavy they heard a loud knocking at the door. "Shit," he cursed and jumped off her and grabbed his pants, putting them on. "He's early," he said as he grabbed his shirt and headed out, turning back to look at her. "Sorry babe, this will have to wait until later. Get dressed and come join us."

"Shitty timing he has," she said, still feeling the heat between her legs.

Neil was buttoning up his shirt when he opened the door to Roy.

"Looks like I'm interrupting you once again," he said, smiling when he saw Neil doing his shirt up and how flush his face was. "Is Kiara awake? I should talk to both of you."

"Yeah, she's getting dressed and will be out in a minute. I made coffee, do you want one?"

"Yes," he answered and followed Neil into the kitchen. He sat down and took the mug from him when he handed it to him, just then she walked in. He gave her a big smile and said good morning and watched when she kissed Neil before getting herself a cup.

Neil sat with his arm over her shoulder. "So did you search the house and talk to Charlie?"

"By the time we got there the house was empty, everyone was gone, no trace of them. We didn't find anything in the basement, no cages, nothing to show that women were being kept prisoners there."

"But your guys saw the same two men who brought Kiara here going in and out of that house with some women," Neil said, getting upset.

"You had to have found the room with the cages."

"We looked and didn't find anything."

Neil stood up, running his hand over the back of his head. "This is crazy, what about Charlie, what did he have to say when you questioned him?"

"That's just it, he disappeared along with the other men and the women. We're still looking for them but in the meantime, I have an idea." He looks at her. "I'd like for you to come with me to the house, maybe you will remember something else. If we can find that room then we might get some clues as to where they went and if they have the girls with them."

"No fucking way. She's still in danger as long as those pricks are loose and I'm not going to put her in any more danger. How could they leave that house without your men seeing them?"

Roy lowered his head in sadness. "Two of my men were watching the house, both were found with their throats slit. I have to find the people responsible and if that means Kiara has to go back to the house of horrors then so be it. I'll be with her along with my crew."

"I'm sorry about your men but I can't let her go through that."

She placed her hand over his. "Neil, I won't be safe until these men are caught and if going back there will trigger my memory then I have to do it. I have to help save those other women."

He looked at her, he knew deep down she was right. "Alright, but I'm going with you." He looked back at Roy. "How did they know your men were watching the place?"

Roy scratched his chin, looking distraught. "Someone had to have tipped them off. I'm wondering if we have a traitor in the bureau. We are checking out all the men who work for us, I just don't know who to trust. Look, I'm going to go back to the office and set things up. I'll be back in a couple of hours and we'll go to that house. I pray we find something."

When Roy walked out Neil took her into his arms, he was worried about her. "You don't have to do this."

"Oh but I do. I can't go on living this way, being afraid that one day they will take me. I want to live my life in peace, with you. I'm sure they got the right house, but I can't understand how they didn't find the room where the girls are being kept."

"Let's have something to eat before Roy comes back for us, we'll have to go out the back way and through the garage so no one will see us."

After they ate Roy called to say he was in the underground parking lot waiting for them. So putting on the hoodie and wearing sunglasses she held Neil's hand as they went down the stairway.

Roy was with another agent and when he saw them approaching he motioned for them to get in the back. The windows on the van were tinted so that no one could see inside. "Did anyone see you leave with Kiara?" he asked, looking back at them.

"No, we were careful," Neil answered back, looking over at the driver.

Roy noticed and introduced them. "This here is agent William Smith. Don't worry, you can trust him."

Neil sat back and relaxed, holding her hand. "Any word on Charlie yet?"

"We can't find him anywhere, it's like he vanished off the face of the earth. Even the others are nowhere to be found. They're still out there and it's only a matter of time before we find them."

When they got closer to their destination he asked Kiara to close her eyes and to tell them if she recognized any smells and then he rolled down his window.

She closed her eyes, at first she couldn't smell anything but soon the faint odor of fish hit her. "That's it, that the smell," she said, opening her eyes. She knew they were getting close to the house where she was held prisoner and she started to shake.

Roy leaned over the seat and held out a blindfold. "I'd like for you to wear this before we reach the house."

"What the fuck for?" Neil snapped, he wasn't sure what Roy was up to.

He looked at her. "I know this is scary for you. But we find that if a victim repeats step by step what they went through, the way they went through it they are able to remember more, such as smells, how many steps they took, and a feeling of what room they were in. It might help you to show us the way to where you and the others were kept. We couldn't find the secret room but blindfolded you might be able to."

She takes the blindfold and hands it to Neil. "It's worth a try, put it on me."

He did as she asked, knowing she was scared out of her mind.

They stopped when they reached the house and they all got out of the van. "Now Neil and I will walk you in the way those men did. Just take your time and if you think of anything let me know, no matter how small it might seem."

William pulled out his gun and led the way as the other two held onto her arm and walked her up the stairs and went inside.

"Are you getting the sense of anything?"

Her lips began to tremble, the smell hit her nose hard, it was just like she remembered, quiet but smelled musty. "We walked straight ahead a few steps then turned right. I remember hearing something being moved, it must have been heavy because two men were groaning and then I could hear a door being opened."

The men all looked around but saw nothing that resembled a door. "There's no door here, just an old grandfather's clock,"

William said as he checked it out."

"Let's move it, maybe there's something behind it," Roy said and then he and William started moving it, it made a weird scraping noise.

"I know that sound, it made it when I was waiting for them to do whatever they were doing," she said, a cold chill going through her.

Once the clock was moved they still didn't see anything out of the ordinary. "There's nothing, just a wall" Roy swore. "Wait, what's this?" he asked, running his hand over a crack in the wall and when he pushed it the wall opened up, revealing a door, both Roy and William stared at each other.

"Damn, how did we miss this the first time we were here?" William said, frowning.

They opened the door and taking her arm led her down the stairs. When they reached the bottom and looked around after turning on the lights William again cursed. "Shit, this is the same basement we were in when we searched the place, only a different way in."

"No, I remember going down more stairs," she said, removing her blindfold.

"There are no more stairs, we searched it inch by inch."
"I'm telling you there is, maybe it's hidden behind another wall, or on the floor." She looked up at Neil. "I know this is the place they took me to, the sounds and smells, this is it."
"I believe you, sweetheart."
Roy went and stood in front of her. “Kiara, you were scared and under a lot of stress. Isn't it possible you misjudged how many stairs you went down?"
"No," she answered, shaking her head.
"Roy, I believe her and since we're here let's do our own search."
"He looked at him. “Alright Neil, no harm in taking another look."
"Boss, do you want me to call for backup?"
"Not yet, not until we find something." Just then his phone rang so he answered, after talking for a few minutes he hung up and swore. "Fuck, that was headquarters, the Sex Kitten site has been closed, and now there's no way of tracing them and we were close to finding out where it was coming from."
"So what does that mean, is the investigation over?" Neil asked, feeling more frustrated than ever. If that were the case she could still be in danger and they would have to be looking over their shoulders for the rest of their lives, or go into the witness program.
"It means that it's going to be harder finding them, they are sure to start up again under a different

name. I'm not giving up on this case, we can still find Charlie and when we do we'll get the answers we need. Let's start looking for another set of stairs, check every corner, every wall, there has to be something here."

Each one, even Kiara, started going over to the basement and after three hours they were starting to lose all hope. After tearing up the place and moving everything away from the walls and even checking for a trap door on the floor they were ready to give up.

Covered in dirt and cobwebs William lit up a cigarette. "We're not going to find anything," he said and leaned up against an old wood stove.

Being a big guy and the way he slammed back into it jolted it, causing it to move an inch and behind it, the wall separated. They all looked from one to the other, their mouths dropped open, and moved closer.

"I'll be damned, whoever built this house sure liked having secret doors," Willian said, dropping his cigarette and stomping it out. He then with the help of the others opened it wider, finding a light switch they turned it on.

"There are stairs leading down," Roy said, looking over at her. "You were right, let's go check it out."

Neil grabbed her arm before she could take the first step. "No, I want you to stay here."

"But Neil," she started to say but Roy interrupted her.

"He's right, it's better you stay here, we don't know what's down there."

The three men descended the stairs, both FBI agents taking out their guns and aiming as they went down. There were only a few steps when they found another door that once had locks on it but now lay on the ground. Neil opened it as the other two aimed their weapons. Once inside they froze, the agents lowered their guns and looked around.

They turned back around when they heard a scream and just in time to see Kiara covering her mouth before she fainted.

Chapter 12

Neil raced to her side, he got to her before her head hit the cement floor. Putting his hand under her head he stroked her hair. "Kiara, wake up baby." He let out a sigh of relief when her eyes fluttered open.

"Get her out of here now," Roy said, squatting down next to her.

Neil didn't need to be told twice, she had already seen too much and he didn't want her to see the rest. Scooping her up into his arms carried her up the narrow stairs. He then took her outside into the fresh air and laid her down on the grass.

As they walked down the stairs William and Roy first aimed their guns. The stench was almost unbearable, a mixture of blood and urine. Stepping into the room they stopped dead in their tracks when they saw the sight before them. A dozen women, naked and some half-naked lay on the ground in a pool of their own blood. When Kiara screamed they turned in time to see her faint. He ordered Neil to take her out before he and William checked out the place and the bodies.

"Boss, you better come here," William shouted out.

He walked over to where William was and there lying were the two men who had been the ones who brought Kiara to Neil, both dead with a bullet in their heads. "Better call it in." He leaned against the wall, just seeing all those women dead, and one couldn't have been more than fourteen made him want to throw up. He had to get out of there so he left the basement and headed outside to see how Kiara was doing.

Walking over he finds her in Neil's arms, her face buried in his chest. "How is she doing?" he asked, getting down to their level.

"I think she's in shock, I should get her home."

"The police are on their way and as soon as they get here I'll drive you. Neil, the two men who brought her to you are also in there, both dead. We have to find this Charlie guy, until then Kiara is still in danger so I'm going to have a man watching over you both."

"But if everyone is dead and the site shuts down, why would she still be in danger?"

"People like this don't like to leave any loose ends, they'll want to get rid of anything or anyone who might be able to identify them."

Neil's eyes grew wide and he stared at Roy. "My God, Eric could also be in danger since they think she's with him."

Roy's eyebrows furrowed together. Standing up he took out his phone and told the person on the other end to go have a word with him and let him know the situation and that he would be put under protection. "I'm having someone keep watch over him, he'll be safe but I'm sure by now the boss of the operation knows she's with you and not Eric."

He kissed the top of her head, and the guilt swept through him, leaving a burning pain in his heart. "I've put my best friend in danger, I never should have gotten him involved in all of this. I'll never forgive myself if anything happens to him."

"Neil, we both know how smart and strong Eric is. You both trained in the art of self-defense and he's one of the best shooters I've ever known. He can take care of himself and he wouldn't have done it if he wasn't capable of handling anything that comes along. Alright, my men are here, just give me a few minutes with them, and then we'll leave."

When Roy left them Neil leaned over to kiss her cheek which was covered in dirt but he didn't care. "We're going home now." He was worried as he held her, she had stopped crying and was so quiet. It was like she had tuned out, she just stared back at him with vacant eyes. He picked her up and carried her over to the van when he saw Roy waving him over. Her arms went around his neck, holding on for dear life. He placed her in the back seat and got in next to her where she snuggled up, putting her arms back around his neck.

"I'll assign a man to watch over you both until we solve the case," Roy said as he pulled into the underground parking lot of Neil's hotel. He then went up with them, making sure they got inside alright.

Once they were alone he took her into his arms, she still hadn't spoken and he was getting worried, knowing she had to let it out for her to start feeling better. "Do you want to talk about what happened?"

"No, I want to take a shower."

"Alright, you go ahead, I'll join you in a minute, there's something I need to do."

She walks away, not bothering to ask him what that was. Turning the water on she strips off her clothes and gets in, letting the water run down her, washing away the dirt and grime. She felt numb inside and when he came into the shower she went into his open arms. Pushing the scene of what went down earlier she let him comfort her, feeling safe in his arms.

After they washed up he turned off the water and stepped out, wrapping a towel around his waist and then putting one around her.

She goes over to the sink and looking in the mirror picks up the hairbrush, but feels too weak to brush her hair. Still staring into the mirror she feels him taking the brush from her and he starts brushing her hair. She watched as he then grabs the hairdryer and blows dry her hair. She had never heard of a man doing something like this before and it felt good the way he was tending to her.

He was glad that she didn't push him away when he held her, the water running down their bodies. He had no thoughts about making love to her, he just wanted to comfort her. He just wished she would open up, scream, cry, anything but keeping it bottled up inside her. "I'll make us something to eat," he said once her hair was dried and he again brushed it for her. Taking her hand he takes her into the bedroom and gets her a nightgown to put on, he then puts on a pair of jeans.

"I'm not hungry," she said, slipping the gown on.

"You have to eat something, now come on, let's get you settled on the couch. I think there's a good movie coming on."

Getting her covered up on the sofa he turns on the movie channel, finding a romantic comedy for them to watch. Leaving her with a glass of wine went into the kitchen and started making them some hamburgers and a tossed salad. Putting them on plates he carried them into the living room, he figured they would eat in front of the TV. It tugged on his heartstrings to see her sitting there, her face so pale and she had this look of doom on her face.

He sits down next to her, holding her plate up. "I put on all your favorite ingredients on your burger. Please try and eat something for me."

She looks at the plate and slowly takes it from him. "Thank you, it does look and smell good. I guess I could eat a little." Taking the first bite was all it took, she realized how hungry she was and started eating until it was all gone, then she started on the salad.

Later he took the plates away and came back with ice cream, he had once heard it was comfort food for women when they were feeling down and hurting. “Is that a small smile I see on your face?" he asked when he handed her the bowl of strawberry ice cream.

"You remembered my favorite kind, thank you," she said, taking it from his hand.

"I listen," he answered as they both dug in.

Even though it was getting late she didn't want to go to bed, she was afraid to close her eyes in case the picture of those girls laying dead came back. If only she could erase it from her memory, to forget the horror of it all. But when he got up, took her hand, and pulled her up she didn't resist when they went to bed. She was relieved when he didn't put the moves on her, she wasn't in the mood for sex. She rested her head on his chest and snuggled up to him, feeling his arm going around her.

His hand rested on her head, every now and then giving it a loving rub. Her hair felt so silky and soft on his skin. He rubbed his thumb over her shoulder, waiting for her to fall asleep, he knew she was fighting it. Once he knew she was out for the count he closed his eyes and went to sleep, hoping that by tomorrow she would be up to talking about what went down.

"Morning:

He woke and quietly slipped out of bed, not wanting to wake her. Grabbing his pants he puts them on as he heads to the kitchen to start the coffee. He had finished putting the grounds into the machine, turned it on, and was reaching for two mugs when he heard her screaming. Forgetting about the cups he ran towards the bedroom, she was still asleep but was having a nightmare, her body thrashing under the covers.

He rushes over and gives her a light shake. "Kiara, it's alright, you're here with me, you're safe," he said, pulling her into his arms. He held her while she cried, letting it all out.

"Oh God, I keep seeing all those girls laying in blood. Why did they have to kill them, why not just let them go or take them somewhere else? I could have been one of them, I could be dead right now if it wasn't for you. One was only fourteen, so young, and had her whole life ahead of her, they didn't have to kill her. When is this going to end?" she asked, sobbing into his shoulder.

"I don't know," he said, holding her against him. He let her cry it out, glad she was finally dealing with it. Once she had settled down he took her into the kitchen and poured her some coffee while he prepared breakfast. "I need to go down to my office and do some work, why don't you get dressed and come with me?"

"Will it be alright for us to be seen together?"

"It's probably known by now that you're not with Eric, and we do have an agent watching over us so yeah, it'll be alright. Besides, I'm not leaving you here alone."

She knew he was right, now with the site having been shut down, they would have checked to see if she was still with Eric. Which meant they would be looking for her and she would feel safer with Neil rather than staying in the suite. "So they will be after me, won't they?"

"Maybe, and again maybe if they packed up and left town they might just leave you alone. I don't really see you being a threat to them anymore. It's not like you know who the boss or bosses are. But to be on the safe side I want you close to me at all times. Once they find Charlie and they get a confession out of him then you'll be free."

As promised he took her down with him and even put her to work, due to her request. She did some filing and he had her type out some memo's for him and showed her how to send them to the people they needed to go to. At noon he called the kitchen and had them send some lunch to his office. While he continued working she went and checked out some of the courses she would be taking to upgrade her education.

Shortly afterward a beautiful brunette walked in carrying a tray of sandwiches and coffee, she set it down and smiled at Neil. "If there's anything else sir just let me know."

"No, that's all Mia. I'd like you to meet my girlfriend, Kiara Finn."

Mia gave him another smile and touched his arm when she looked over at Kiara. "I didn't know you were dating someone." She then turned to her and held out her hand. "It's a pleasure to meet you, Miss Finn."

"Same here," she said, shaking Mia's hand and feeling a twinge of jealousy.

When the woman walked out she turned to Neil. "She was quite touchy with you, should I be worried about the two of you?"

He got up and going around his desk drew her close to him. "She's married so you have nothing to worry about."

"She wouldn't be the first woman to cheat on her husband."

"Baby, she's not only married but she's married to a woman."

She lowered her head and smiled, feeling foolish. "Oh."

He lifted her chin up so that she would have to look at him. "You never have to feel jealous, I know and will always have eyes only for you. I may be a lot of things but I'm not a cheater. Now we could eat our lunch or take off our clothes and lay down on the couch and make out. Your choice."

Walking away she goes over and locks the door. "I've made my choice."

Taking off his shirt and tie he picked up his phone, telling the person on the other end to hold all his calls and that he was not to be disturbed for the next hour. Putting his phone down he motioned with his finger for her to come closer. When she got close he picked her up and sat her down on his desk, pushing everything out of the way. His lips were kept busy on her neck as his fingers worked on undoing the buttons on her blouse. Once it was open he started kissing down her neck to the top of her breasts, he lowered her back down onto the desk. He hiked her skirt up and pulled down her panties. Sitting down in his chair he pushed her legs open and his mouth devoured her, making her squirm and moan. He was so hard and wanted them to come at the same time so he stopped, dropped his pants and lifted her legs up over his shoulders, and began thrusting hard inside her. Her warmth tightened around his member and he couldn't hold back another second. They never made it to the sofa, instead, they satisfied their lust right on his desk.

They cleaned up afterward and he couldn't stop smiling. He had always wondered what it would be like to have office sex and now he knew, it was amazing. Unlocking the door they ate lunch but the coffee had gotten cold so he took out some bottles of water for them from the mini-fridge.

With the work finished he took her with him when he made his rounds, making sure everything was running smoothly. With his arm around her waist, he introduced her to more of his staff as his girlfriend. He figured it was time they met her since he planned on making her his wife someday. They then went back up to the suite and he was glad that she was doing better, she wasn't as upset as she had been after coming back from the house of horrors.

Getting a phone call from Eric he tells her that he was coming over after supper, saying that he wanted to know if he could hang out for a while.

"Is he alright?" she asked as she started preparing dinner.

"He sounded a little down and said he had something to tell me. He has been off lately, I think maybe it has something to do with work."

She turned to look at him. "Oh God, I feel so bad, I've never asked him what he does for a living. I've been so wrapped up in you and my problems I didn't think to ask. What is it that he does for a living?"

"He's a financial adviser, he's really good at it but I think he's bored and might be looking for something else to do with his life. I once offered him a job as my hotel manager but he turned it down."

"Why don't you call him back and invite him to dinner, maybe you can cheer him up."

"You wouldn't mind?"

"Of course not, he's your friend."

"OK, I'll call him now."

An hour later Eric showed up, carrying a bouquet of flowers. He put his arms around her in a hug. "I'm so sorry for what happened to you, you never should have witnessed what you did," he said, releasing her. "I know this won't take away your pain but I got these flowers to help brighten up your day."

"How do you know what happened?" Neil asked.

"Roy told me when he called and now I have an agent keeping watch on me. As if I can't take care of myself," he said, handing her the flowers.

Touched by his kindness she takes them from him. "Thank you, they're beautiful. You guys go sit down and I'll put these in some water. Can I get you something to drink?"

"I could go for a beer."

"Me too," Neil said as they went into the living room.

She came back a few minutes later and handed them the bottles. "I'm just going to finish dinner, it should be ready in about half an hour."

Eric watched the way Neil touched her arm in a loving gesture and the way they looked at each other as she walked away. "You really are in love with her."

"Yes, with every fiber of my being. Kiara is not only a part of my life, but she is also my life. I know someday you'll find a woman to love, one who will give you her heart. I'm telling you, there's nothing better than being in love. I would give my life to save hers."

"I'm sure you'll be happy together and have lots of babies," he said, winking at Neil.

"Dinner's ready," she called out from the dining room where she had everything ready. "I've made roasted chicken and all the trimmings."

"Is that homemade apple pie I smell?" Eric asked, smiling as he loaded up his plate.

"It is," she replied.

Neil reached for the gravy and looked at him. "You said you had something to tell me, do you want to tell me now?"

"I have decided to make a big change in my life, I'm moving to Chicago."

"You're what?"

He looked at Neil who had a stunned look on his face. "You know I haven't been happy with my job and there's nothing here for me. I need a change, a new job, and a different life. I have nothing here."

"You have me, and Kiara. Shit Eric, we have been friends for years."

"We'll still be friends, besides, you have a beautiful woman that loves you, you don't need me hanging around."

"That's not true. Just because I'm with someone doesn't mean I don't want you around. Shit man, we've been through so much together. I can't imagine my life without you in it. Just take your time, don't decide on anything yet."

"Sorry Neil, I'm leaving at the end of the week."

"Why so soon?"

"I've been thinking of it for some time now, I'm ready to make the move. I even got a job lined up with a big company, more money and they are even throwing in an apartment. I'm being given an expense allowance. I never got anything like that here."

"Well, if this is what you want then I'm happy for you."

"Thanks, and don't worry, I'll keep in touch with you and this beautiful lady here."

Afterward, they went and settled in the living room to have a drink and talk.

Eric sat back, crossed his right leg over his left one, and took a swallow of his beer. "So I guess since that site has been closed the investigation is over and Roy said they can't find Charlie anywhere."

"Nope, he's going to keep looking for him, and knowing my brother-in-law he won't stop until he does."

"But Kiara is in the clear though. I mean they would be stupid to come after her, what would be the point? she knows nothing," he said, glancing over at her.

"As long as Charlie is still out there she still could be in danger."

"They'll never find him."

He looked at Eric, his eyebrows shot up. "Why would you say that?"

"I'm just guessing. I mean the man is obviously smart if he was able to run such an organization and dispose of all those people without getting caught. I wouldn't be surprised if he's on the other end of the world by now."

"Yeah, you're probably right," he said, leaning back and putting his arm over her shoulder. "Let's have a few more drinks and celebrate your new job and life."

Roy was sitting in his office after calling his wife to let her know he'd be late and not to hold dinner. This latest case was giving him gray hairs, with the site shut down and no sign of Charlie he wasn't sure if it would ever get solved. He looked up when there was a knock at his door and saw a grinning William looking down at him.

"I've got great news for you boss."

"Good, I could use some."

"Charlie Richards has been found and is being brought in now."

Roy jumped to his feet. "We got the bastard, but I really think he's not working alone. We need to get him to tell us who he's working with. Let me call Neil and tell him the good news." Picking up his phone he dialed his number.

"Neil, it's me, I have some great news for you. Charlie has been caught and he'll be here soon."

That's great, so it's all over.

"Not yet. I believe he has a partner and I'm going to find out who. I just wanted to let you know and when I get him to talk I'll call you back so hang tight.

Thanks for letting me know, I'll tell Kiara, she'll be relieved.

Roy hung up, he was anxious to interrogate Charlie. He grabbed a cup of coffee and headed to the interrogation room where Charlie was cuffed to the metal table, sporting a smirk on his face.

He and William sat down across from him. "Mr. Richards, we've been looking for you for a long time now."

"So you got me, now what?"

"We know you are the owner of the Sex Kitten site, an illegal site that promotes the prostitution of girls that you kidnapped and forced to perform sex with the clients. You're going to spend the rest of your life in prison."

"My lawyer will get me off."

"Not that simple pal. You're also going down for murder, we found all the dead girls and the two men you had working for you." He leaned over, getting in the man's face. "You're not smart enough to pull this off by yourself, who are you working with?"

"I didn't do anything and you can't prove it."

"We have your DNA from the house and pictures of you going in and out on several different occasions.

Charlie started to squirm, his face turned red.

"Come on man, we know you helped to kidnap those girls. You had Kiara snatched and put into the site when she refused to have a threeway with you and a buddy."

"That bitch was no fun so I kicked her out but I didn't have her taken, or anyone for that matter."

Roy banged his fist on the table. "Look you a little piece of shit, we know it was you. We have enough evidence to put you away. Think about it, while you're rotting in prison your partner is walking around free, enjoying the good life. If you think he will lift a hand to help you think again. I bet he has already made plans to start up again somewhere else, leaving you here to rot."

Charlie was starting to sweat, he got to thinking about how his boss treated him like dirt, ordering him around and making him feel stupid. If it wasn't for the man's connections and how he arranged everything he would have told him to go fuck himself. For two years they had a good run and made more money than he ever dreamed of. But because of that bitch, Kiara, and her newfound boyfriend whose brother-in-law just happened to be an FBI agent, it all started to go to hell. He was also sure that the man would be far gone soon and he wasn't about to take the wrap alone.

"What's it going to be Charlie?"

"If I tell you what kind of deal will you give me?"

Roy looked at William and shook his head. "The man's a killer and kidnapper and he wants a deal."

"Maybe if he gives up the name of his boss maybe we can give him a break."

Roy turned back to Charlie. "The best we can do is tell the court you cooperated with us, they just might go a little easier on you, now give me his name."

"Eric, Eric Hopkins."

Roy's face turned pale and his jaw dropped open.

Going back before Roy talked to Charlie: Neil had his back to the other two as he hung up the phone. "They've got Charlie so it's only a matter of time before he tells them who the mastermind behind the site is." He turned around and stopped breathing when he saw Eric with his arm over Kiara's neck and the barrel of a gun pressed against her temple.

Chapter 13

His eyes went as wide as saucers when he saw Eric pointing a gun at her head. "Eric, what are you doing? Please, put the gun down, let's discuss this." He looked into her eyes which were filled with tears when she looked back into his eyes.

"I'm really sorry about this Neil. If only that sniveling coward Charlie had left town when I told him all of this could have been avoided. I didn't want any of this but I have no choice, if only you hadn't found that damn site."

When he tried to move toward them Eric pressed the gun harder into her temple, causing him to stand still." Oh God, I can't believe you are involved in this. Why Eric?"

"Why, you want to know why? I'll tell you why. I'm so sick of being the poor friend of the great Neil Hicks. I want to be rich too and thanks to this site I have made millions of dollars. You've always gotten everything you wanted, this hotel, the women, and money. You were born with a silver spoon in your mouth, everything was given to you while I had to bust my ass off just to pay my bills."

"Is this what it's all about, are you jealous of me?"

"Not of you, just of everything you have, I want it too."

"Eric, you and I have been friends since we were four years old, we've been through a lot and I think of you as a brother. What you've done, all those poor women you murdered, how could you?"

"I didn't kill them, Charlie and the other two men did, and then he killed the men. Charlie was the one who found all the women for me."

"You're as much to blame as he is. You have to give yourself up, it's the only way."

Eric kissed Kiara's head, smelling her hair as he did it. "When I found you that day when you went on the site I was shocked at first. Then I got to thinking, why not let you have some fun, what harm could it do? But then you had to go and fall in love with her. I don't blame you though, there is something about her, even though I really like her."

"Then let her go," he said, begging him as he looked at her. "Charlie will end up telling the cops about you, it's over."

"Yeah, I'm sure it's only a matter of time before that meddling brother-in-law of yours breaks him. But by then I'll be long gone. I came here tonight to say goodbye, I was going to leave you both alone to be happy together. Charlie was supposed to have left the country then no one would have known about me, we all could have lived a good life and no one would be the wiser."

"It's not too late, just let us go, we won't call the cops."

Eric was starting to sweat, his hold around her neck tightening. "It's too late, it's only a matter of time before Charlie spills his guts, so now I have to go into hiding."

"What are you planning on doing with us?"

"I'm sorry, I can't let you live, you know that. Neil, I'm so sorry."

"Eric, wait," he shouted out, holding up his hands. "I know you have feelings for Kiara, I've seen it in your eyes and the way you look at her. Let her live, take her with you, make her yours." His shirt was soaked with sweat, he was wondering what was taking Roy so long, he had to keep stalling Eric.

Eric placed his lips against her ear. "How about it sweetheart, would you be willing to come with me, be my bitch?"

"Tell him you'll go and you'll do whatever he wants," Neil said, begging with his eyes for her to agree.

He stared into her eyes, praying that she would go along with it.

She stared back at him, tears falling down her face, she knew he wanted her to agree. "Yes, yes I'll go with you, whatever you want. But you have to let him live, then I'll not give you any trouble." If it meant that Neil would live then she would do whatever it took, even leaving the only man she would ever love.

"That's so touching but I can't, you both have to die." He looks at Neil. "I'm sorry bro, I really am, please forgive me." He pointed the gun at him, shooting him right in the chest. He lost his grip on her when she struggled and ran to Neil. As she was bending over him sobbing, Eric aimed the gun at her. "I'm sorry Kiara."

But before he could take the shot that would end her life the door was kicked in and Roy, aiming his weapon, shot Eric in the head, killing him.

***

Now we will backtrack before the shooting:

The first thing Roy did when he found out Eric was the boss behind the site he called the guards who were protecting them. When he got no answer he called Neil, getting no answer he knew something was wrong. He called for backup, saying for them to meet him at the hotel. The guards were nowhere in sight and when he got his hands on them they would be looking for new jobs. His mind kept going over what all Charlie had told him, how Eric was the ringleader and hired men to do the dirty work. His mind was going a hundred miles an hour, he had known Eric for many years and never once suspected him of being capable of doing such a crime. He was Neil's best friend, surely he wouldn't hurt him. What he found when he kicked in the door to Neil's suite had his blood freezing in his veins, he had no choice but to shoot when he saw that Eric's gun was aimed at Kiara and he was ready to pull the trigger.

**

He pulled the trigger, hitting Eric in the head, he dropped like a sack of potatoes as blood gushed from his temple. He ran over to Neil and saw blood oozing from his chest, judging from where the bullet went he knew it wasn't good. Kiara was sobbing over his body, pressing a towel on his wound. He called for an ambulance and got on his knees. "Neil, stay with us buddy, help is on its way." He saw his eyes flutter open but as they looked at her, he could see life draining from his eyes. "Keep talking to him, let him know you're here," he said, trying to hold back his own tears.

"Neil, stay with me sweetheart, I love you. Don't you leave me, I need you, we need you," she said, touching his face with one hand while the other one held the towel on his wound. When she noticed him looking at her as he tried to keep his eyes open she nodded her head. "I'm pregnant, we're having a baby so you hang on." She leaned over, kissing his lips ever so softly. "Fight to stay alive, for us."

Roy was speechless when he heard what she said to him. But he wasn't sure if she was just saying that to get him to fight harder to live or if she really was pregnant. Either way, it didn't matter as long as it worked. He looked at his watch, wondering what was taking the ambulance so long, he went over to check on Eric. He already knew the man was dead but he had to double-check.

When the ambulance arrived he rode in it with her, he wasn't sure how he was going to tell Judy what had happened. But knew he had to call her once they reached the hospital and knew she was going to be furious with him for not telling her about it earlier. Though it was their rule that he wouldn't discuss his cases until they were over, this was different, it was family.

She kept wiping his forehead with a cloth. "I'm here, I'm never going to leave your side. You fight Neil, you fight to stay alive." She didn't know if he could hear her or not, but she was going to keep talking, hoping he would. Her heart beat wildly inside her chest when he opened his eyes a couple of times and then closed them again. When they arrived at the hospital she tried to go with him when they took him into the operating room. Roy had to hold her back as she tried to break free, saying she had to be with him, her sobs loud when he disappeared through the door.

"Kiara, let's sit down and let them do their job," he said, his arm around her, leading her over to one of the chairs. "I have to call Judy and let her know what happened, you stay right here." Getting up he walks over to the wall and takes out his phone. It broke his heart to hear his wife cry when he told her it didn't look good. Hanging up he went and sat back down beside her.

She looked at the blood on her hands, her clothes were also covered in his blood. "He's going to make it isn't he?"

He waved a nurse over and asked for a wet cloth and towel. "They are doing everything they can for him, we have to have faith that he'll survive." Taking the wet cloth from the older nurse he starts cleaning her hands and the blood from her face. "I know this is a bad time but can you tell me what Eric said before he shot Neil?"

Through bursts of sobs, she told him everything that she could remember. "He also said that he was going to leave, and let us have a life together but then he heard that Charlie was caught and knew he would rat him out. So he figured he had to kill us too. How could he try to kill his best friend, the thing is he did look remorseful."

"I'm sure a big part of him hated what he was going to do, they were so close. Each one had the other's back when it came to a fight. I remember when I first started seeing Judy Neil come to see me, he punched me and said I better treat her right or he'd be back to beat the shit out of me. I was in my second year as an FBI agent, he could have been arrested. Eric was with him and he glared at me and said he'd be more than happy to help Neil. I can't believe he wanted to kill him."

"I can't lose him," she said and started to cry.

He put his arms around her, comforting her until he saw the nurse approaching them. He stood up and so did she. "Can you tell us anything?" he asked, wishing Judy was with them.

"He's in surgery, the bullet entered his heart and they are going to have to remove it. It's a very delicate operation and could take a few hours."

"But he's going to be alright isn't he?" she asked, holding on to Roy's arm.

"I'm sorry, it's too soon to say. I do suggest that if he has any other family you should call them, and have them come."

"Oh my God, I know what that means, you don't think he's going to live," she cried out, falling back into her chair as she started bawling. She felt Roy's arms going around her. "They're wrong, he's going to live because without him I won't be able to."

He lifted her head up so that he could look into her eyes to see the truth. "If you were telling the truth earlier about being pregnant with his child then you will live on, for his sake as well as his child."

"I am pregnant. I didn't know it until that night when Eric and Neil were in the living room having a drink. I had one and felt ill, so I went and threw up. I haven't taken a test but I know I'm pregnant."

"Yeah, Judy knew she was too before she took one of those tests. I'm glad you told him, it just might be the thing that will make him fight. Kiara, if I had known Eric was at your place I never would have said anything over the phone, I would have just come over."

"It's not your fault, you had no way of knowing he was with us. If anyone is to be blamed it's me."

"How so?" he asked, wondering what she was getting at.

"If he hadn't met me none of this would have happened, he wouldn't be in there fighting for his life. I'm the one who should be laying there, not Neil."

"Now you stop with this nonsense, he's the one that ordered you from that site. It's no one's fault. There's no excuse for what Eric did and Neil would be so mad at you if he heard you talking this way." He looked up when he heard Judy's voice call out to him. Letting go of Kiara he got up, pulling his wife into his arms.

Judy's face was all blotchy, her nose was running so she wiped it with a tissue. "What happened, how is Neil?" she asked, her tears falling as she looked over at Kiara.

He took her face in his hands. "Honey, I will explain everything later, but now is not the time. He's in surgery and it doesn't look good. The nurse says it will be a few hours so have a seat, maybe you could take Kiara somewhere to change her clothes. She's really in a bad way right now, she could use a friend."

Judy went and sat down, taking Kiara's hand in hers. "Hey, my brother is strong and way too stubborn to give up, he'll pull through this. Let's go into the washroom and get you cleaned up, you wouldn't want him seeing you looking this way now, would you? I brought you some of my things, we're the same size so I know they will fit you."

"OK," she said, following Judy into the nearest bathroom. Taking off the bloody clothes she washed her hands and face before putting on the jeans and top that Judy handed her. "Thank you."

"I don't know the whole story yet but I'm glad you're alright," she said, then gave her a big hug before they went back out into the waiting room. She was glad to see that Roy had gone and got them some coffee.

Roy sat next to his wife. "Where's Chrissy?"

"At the neighbor's place, she's going to spend the night there. I didn't tell her that her uncle was in the hospital, I didn't want her to worry."

Kiara sat with her hands folded, her head hung down. She didn't want to close her eyes in case she saw what had taken place, the look on Neil's face when he was shot would haunt her for the rest of her life. It was a mixture of shock, pain, and utter horror. "What's taking them so long? It's been over four hours."

Neither Roy nor Judy had an answer for her. All they knew was that taking a bullet out of a heart was a difficult and delicate procedure. Five hours later when the doctor walked out with blood on his top they all got to their feet.

"How is my brother?" Judy asked, trying her best to hold back her tears.

"He survived the operation but he's not out of the woods yet. All we can do is wait and pray. I'm sorry but I have to tell you I'm not sure he will make it, I'm so sorry. You can go see him as soon as he's taken to his room."

"You don't know him as I do, my brother is a fighter." She turned to Kiara. "He will live, you have to believe that."

"I do," she said, wiping away her tears.

An hour later they were shown to his room, Kiara was the first one to enter. She walked slowly towards the bed, his chest was bare except for the bandage on his chest, covering the bullet wound. It felt like someone had punched her hard in the stomach when she saw all the wires and hookups attached to his body. His eyes were closed, his face so pale and his breathing shallow. There is nothing worse than seeing the one you love laying lifeless in a hospital bed, knowing that at any moment they might take their last breath.

Going over she takes his hand in hers, lifting it to her lips as she pressed them gently against his skin. "Neil, I'm here sweetheart. I love you, please stay with me."

The other two stood on the other side of the bed, Judy moved his hair from his forehead. "Hey big brother, I love you," she said as she shed some tears.

After two hours Roy went and got them all something to drink, he pulled up a chair for her so that she could sit by his bed. He and Judy went over by the window, sat down, and watched Kiara as she kept holding his hand and talking to him. It wasn't about anything in particular, just everyday stuff. They all looked up when the doctor walked in, carrying his chart.

"Hello, I'm Doctor Sands, I'm just going to have a look here." After examining him he smiled at the others. "His signs are stable, that's a good sign.

Kiara stared at the doctor, her hope rising. "So is he going to be alright?"

"I have to be honest with you, he's not out of the woods yet. The first twenty-four to forty-eight hours are critical. All you can do is wait, talk to him and let him know you're here. But it's going to be a long wait, I suggest some of you go home and get some rest. We'll call you if there are any changes in his condition."

She shakes her head. "I'm not leaving him."

A few hours later Roy decided to take Judy home, he knew she was exhausted from worry. He tried to convince Kiara to go with them but when she refused he went and got her a blanket and pillow. "At least try to get some sleep."

"I will," she answers, putting the pillow behind her back and covering herself with the blanket. Nothing was going to get her to leave Neil's side. When they were gone she kept hold of his hand and talked to him. Soon she rested her head on the edge of the bed and closed her eyes. She kept waking up to give him soft kisses on the lips and telling him how much she loved him.

Early the next day Roy and Judy showed up, with them there were bagels, tea, and some fresh fruit for Kiara. Judy went over and kneeled before her. "Roy told me that you think you might be pregnant so I stopped and bought you one of those pregnancy tests. Would you like to take it now?"

At first, she didn't want to. It would mean leaving his bedside, even if it was only for a few minutes. Then when she gave it some thought she nodded, she took the box from Judy and went into the bathroom. A few minutes later she came back into the room and back over to Neil. "It will take five minutes for the results."

Five minutes later Judy stood up. "It's time, are you going to check it?"

"I don't want to leave his side, you can check it if you want to."

Judy came back from the bathroom, a smile plastered on her face. "It's official, you're two and a half weeks pregnant." She went over and hugged her. "This is a good thing, aren't you happy?"

"We didn't plan on this, but yes." She touched her stomach. "I'm having Neil's baby and I couldn't be happier." She turned and leaned over him, tenderly touching his cheek. "You hear that sweetheart, we are having a baby. I love you so much."

The other two convinced her to sit down and eat, saying she had to take care of herself for the sake of the baby. By the time Roy and Judy were getting ready to leave he went and arranged for a cot to be brought into the room, then said they'd be back later with something for her to eat. No matter how hard they tried they couldn't talk her into leaving with them.

For five days and nights, she never left his side even though the doctors had said he had slipped into a coma. But they were hopeful of his recovery, saying that being in the coma was the body's way of dealing with what had happened to him. Since he was still alive after the two days they were sure he would wake up soon and they were all encouraged to keep talking to him. She kept busy reading to him, giving him sponge baths. She even ate the food the hospital brought to her.

She had just finished shaving his face when Judy dropped in. "It's a good thing he's not awake, he would never let anyone shave him," she said, walking over to the bed with a smile on her face.

Kiara turned to her. "I know by now Roy must have told you how Neil and I met. I hope you don't think too badly of me. But I want you to know that I love him, he is the most wonderful man I have ever known."

"I was shocked at first, that is until Roy explained everything. What you went through, no one should ever have had to go through. I'm glad Neil found you first and I know you love him, the same way I know he loves you. But it's all behind you now, you're pregnant and I know once he wakes up he is going to be thrilled to bits." She gave Kiara a hug, feeling sad for all that the young woman had to endure in her short life.

When Roy showed up she was able to convince Kiara to go out with her to a nearby restaurant for a decent meal. But she only agreed if Roy stayed with Neil and promised to call them if he so much as blinked. She had to admit to Judy that it did feel good getting away from the hospital but she still wanted to hurry back.

Later when she was alone with Neil she started to change his bandage. She had insisted they show her how so that once he was better she could do it when they went back home. She felt her heart breaking when she saw the scar and wished he would wake up. "I wish you would open your eyes, I really need you to come back to me." For the first time in days, she sported a small smile, one full of mischief. She leaned over him, her lips close to his ear. "Maybe if I were to shave you down there you might wake up, that ought to do it."

"Do and I'll spank you."

She straightens up and with her mouth wide open she looks at him, tears filling her eyes. "Neil, you're awake." She leaned back over, covering his face with kisses before she placed her lips softly on his.

He put his hand behind her head, kissing her back.

"I need to let the doctor know you're awake," she said, reaching for the button on his bed that rang for the nurse. "I knew you'd come back to me."

They didn't have time to say anything else when the nurse came in and went over to check him out.

"I'll let the doctor know you're awake," she said and left the room.

He smiled at her, his hand going to her stomach he placed it over her belly. "We're having a baby"

"You heard me tell you?"

"Yes. I can't remember what happened, just that everything went dark and there was so much pain. But I heard you tell me to fight for you both, that you were carrying my baby." Then he touched the side of her face with the palm of his hand. "Thank God you're alright. If anything had happened to you or our baby I don't know what I would have done. What about Eric, where is he?"

"We can talk about that later, right now you need to rest. I have to call Roy and Judy and let them know you're back with us."

His eyes grew heavy and he blinked. "Every time I felt myself slipping away into the darkness I'd hear your voice, calling to me, bringing me back. I'm alive because of you and because you didn't give up on me. I have you and our baby to live for."

Just then the doctor walked in. "Mr. Hicks, it's about time you woke up. So tell me, how are we feeling today?"

"I don't know about you, doctor but I feel like a ton of bricks fell on top of me."

"Let me just examine you. Can you remember anything about what happened to you?" he asked as he checked his vital signs.

"Only that I was shot, don't know when."

"Almost a week now, most of that time you were in a coma. Things look really good but taking the bullet out of your heart has left some scarring on the tissue. You will make a full recovery but it will take time."

"When can I get out of here?"

"Maybe in two weeks, sooner if you take it easy and do what you're told. I have to see other patients but will check on you later. Oh, if I may say you are a lucky man to have such a loving woman. This young lady hasn't left your side and she even took it upon herself to take care of you, changing your dressing and giving you sponge baths. Not many spouses would do that. I see she even gave you a shave. I'll be back later."

He turned his head towards her. "You didn't have to do all that, they have people to do it."

"Do you really think that for one minute I was going to let some pretty young nurse wash your body and your private parts? No way, no how. I have to call your sister now and let her know," she said and going over to the phone picked it up and dialed.

Chapter 14

After talking to Judy she hung up the phone and went to sit by his side. "They will be here tomorrow, it's late and they don't have a sitter for Chrissy but they are so happy that you're awake. To be honest, I'm glad they aren't coming, I want you all to myself." She ran her fingers over his cheek. "I was so worried about you, I thought I was going to lose you."

"Lay down next to me, let me hold you."

She got in next to him, hoping they wouldn't get caught. Laying on her side she put her arm over his stomach, her head resting on the pillow and she looked at him. "Are you really happy about the baby?"

He turned his head to look back at her, she looked so tired, knowing the last few days must have been hard on her. "If I wasn't trapped in this bed I'd be picking you up and swinging you around. I want this baby very much, so yes, I'm extremely happy." He took hold of her hand. "Kiara, I love you. Will you marry me?"

She sat up to get a better look at him. "Neil, are you actually proposing to me now, here in your hospital bed?"

A sleepy grin appeared on his face. "I know this isn't very romantic, I should do it over a more romantic setting. I've been wanting to ask you for some time now and I can't wait any longer."

"You're not just asking because of the baby are you?"

"Sweetheart, you know how I feel about you, your being pregnant has nothing to do with me asking you. I'm sorry, I don't know what I was thinking. I should wait until I can propose to you properly."

"Yes," she said, smiling at him.

"You will?" he asked, taking her hand in his.

"Yes, I'll marry you," she answered, leaning over him as she kissed him. After talking for a while they both finally drifted off to sleep. Being beside him in bed she was able to sleep right through the night.

Judy showed up the next day with more fresh clothes for Kiara to put on, she started bawling when she saw Neil. "You big stupid jerk, what were you thinking getting yourself shot like that?"

"I love you too sis."

She kissed him and wiped her tears away. "Roy will be here soon and Chrissy drew you a picture. She wanted to come but I thought it was too soon, it might scare her seeing you like this."

He took the picture and smiled. "I take it this is me and Kiara, but what is this in my arms?"

"That's mittens you goof, make sure you don't let on to Chrissy that you didn't know that, she'll be crushed."

"I love the drawing, I'll keep it right by the bed."

When Roy finally arrived Neil was determined to find out what had taken place, neither of the women would tell him what went down, all he knew was Eric was dead, but he still didn't know. "OK, Roy, I want you to tell me everything."

"Neil, wait until you get your strength up," Kiara said, worried that the facts would affect his recovery.

"No, I need to know," he said more sharply than he meant to.

"Charlie told us everything, how Eric hired him to find the girls. It was Eric who started the site, he bought that house of horrors under a different name a couple of years back."

"Wait a minute, two years ago he asked me for a loan, and said he wanted to buy some property in Florida. Oh my God, he used the money to buy that house. How could I not have known what he was up to?"

"Eric is or was very smart, a technology expert, he knew how to set up the site without being caught, and he knew how and where to hide things. He had Charlie go with the two men to kill the women, the bigger one thought he was their main man and when he was told to kill the other man Charlie was told to get rid of him too. Eric would have gotten away with it if Charlie had left the country like he was supposed to."

"So who shot and killed Eric?"

"I did. I'm sorry Neil, I had to, he was about to kill Kiara and I couldn't let him do that."

"I know, and I thank you for saving her," he said, taking her hand. "The thing is, when I looked into his eyes I could see how much killing us was hurting him, but he was still going to do it. I thought I knew him, I trusted him alone with her."

"If it makes you feel any better I think he was going to leave you both alone, but since you knew about him he couldn't leave any loose ends."

"What about the men who were watching all of us, where the hell did they disappear to?"

Roy sat down, rubbing his hand over his face. "Both men got a text from me saying the job was over and they were to go home. The thing is I never sent them that text, Eric did and he hacked into their phones and fixed it so that they wouldn't receive any calls or texts. Eric had booked a private plane. My guess is he was planning on leaving that night he came over to your place."

"But he told us he wasn't going until that Friday," Neil said, still confused. He couldn't understand why he would tell them one thing but do another."

"I can't answer that, we'll never know what was going through his mind. If he hadn't been found out he would be living somewhere else, and would have kept in touch with you while living a double life."

Neil closed his eyes, he couldn't help feeling hurt and betrayed by a man who he thought of as a brother. Opening his eyes he was determined to move on, to try and forget Eric, and maybe in time learn to forgive him. "Alright, enough about Eric and what went down. It's time for some happy news." He smiled at Kiara and looked over at the other two. "Last night I asked Kiara to marry me and she said yes."

"Oh that's wonderful, but couldn't you have waited to do it in a more romantic way?" Judy asked, but was still happy and smiling from ear to ear.

"To me, it was perfect," Kiara said, leaning over to kiss him.

"Well it's about time you settled down, you son of a gun," Roy said, going over to shake his hand and hug Kiara.

After a while, the nurse came in and said everyone had to leave, and that he needed his rest.

"I want you to go home with them," he said, pulling her closer to him.

"No, I'm not leaving you."

"Baby, you've been by my side for days and you need a homemade meal and to have a good night's sleep in a proper bed. Remember you're pregnant and have to take care of yourself. I love you but to be honest you will only keep me up with your talking. This way I can also get a good night's sleep."

"Oh, so you're saying I talk too much."

"Sweetheart, I just want to make sure you're alright. I will rest so much better if I know you are being taken care of."

"Alright, one night, then I'm coming back and I'm staying until you get released from here. Before you say anything I don't care how long it takes, this will be the only night I leave your side."

Saying goodbye to Neil, Judy and Roy waited outside the room for Kiara, they wanted to give them a few minutes alone together.

She went and sat on the bed next to him. "I love you, are you sure you don't want me to stay?"

"I just want you to get some rest."

Putting her hands on his shoulders she leaned over and kissed him. It was just meant to be a short tender kiss but he cupped the back of her head with his one hand and deepened the kiss. "I'll be back soon," she said once he let go of her.

When she left the room he closed his eyes. He was already missing her and when he heard the door opening he kept them closed, he didn't want to see anyone but her. But he did open them quickly when he felt someone getting on the bed. "Kiara, what are you doing back here?" He was surprised to find her there but it was a good surprise.

"I changed my mind about leaving and I promise not to talk too much."

He takes her hand, bringing it to his lips. "I'm glad you're here and talk as much as you want. I love the sound of your voice."

The next week went fast, every day she would take him for short walks down the hall and back again. The doctor said he needed to get up and move around, but for only a short time and that he still needed plenty of rest. Judy and Chrissy came to visit him, bringing more drawings for him and some for Kiara which had pictures of a baby in them.

On the tenth day, he was taken in for some tests to make sure there were no problems with his heart from the scaring. When the doctor came in to see him he pulled up a chair and opened his file.

"Mr. Hicks, I'm happy to tell you that everything is fine with your heart. You're young and strong which really helped, so I'm going to release you today. But, and I will stress this, you will have to take it easy for a while. That means more bed rest and no strenuous activities."

Neil looked over at her and smiled. "Looks like you'll have to do all the work for a while," he said and then winked at her.

Her face turned red when he said that in front of the doctor, she wanted to crawl under a rock and hide.

The doctor let out a chuckle. "I'd hold off on that for a while yet. I'll get your discharge papers ready and you can be on your way in a couple of hours. Take care and I want to see you back here in two weeks for a checkup."

"You're so naughty," she said when the doctor was gone. "I'll call Roy to come and pick us up and then I'll get you dressed."

"You've done so much already, why don't you let the nurse dress me?"

She turned to him, crossed her arms, and glared at him. "Not in your life buddy and watch what you say or I'll carry through with my threat to shave you down below and you better hope my hand doesn't slip."

He laughed and held up his hands. "OK, I'm kidding and there's no way you'll ever shave me down there, it's not natural for a man."

"Then behave yourself," she said and called Roy.

In order to avoid his staff and all the questions that they would be sure to ask they went up the back way through the underground parking. After making sure Neil and Kiara were inside their suite he said goodbye, he had to get back to his office.

"OK mister, go into the bedroom and take off your clothes and get into bed."

He went over and put his arms around her waist from behind, his lips going to her neck. "OK, but you'll have to take it easy on me, you heard the doctor."

She turned around to face him, trying to hide a smile. "There will be none of that right now, not until you're up to it. Now go while I make us some lunch." She had felt his manhood pressing against her and knew he was up to it, but because of his heart and what the doctor said she had to stop him.

She went and heated them up some soup and made a couple of sandwiches, putting them on a tray and carrying them into the bedroom. He was sitting up in bed and it hurt her to see him looking so pale and weak. But at least they were home and would be able to sleep in a more comfortable bed, together.

She made sure he ate everything and then went to take the dishes away.

"Wait," he said, holding out his hand to her. "Put that down and come lay with me, you need your rest as much as I do."

It was true, now that she was pregnant she had to take it easy so slipping out of her jeans and top she climbed in next to him, leaving on her bra and panties. She rested her head on his shoulder, she didn't mean to fall asleep so fast but being in his arms pulled her into a sense of security.

He was the first one to wake up so he lay there watching her sleep. It saddened him to think of how close they almost came to losing each other. But they had survived and were expecting a baby, he knew his life couldn't get any better than this.

"Morning sweetheart," he said when she stirred, opening her eyes.

"Morning," she replied, snuggling up to him. "It feels so good being home."

"Yes, it really does, there's nothing like sleeping in one's own bed. Do me a favor babe. Go over to my dresser and in the bottom drawer take out the small bag that's under my jeans." He watched as she got out of bed and went over to the dresser in her underwear.

She finds the bag he was talking about and grabbing it goes back over to the bed, she sees the smirk on his face. "What are you smirking about?" she asked, handing him the package and then getting back into bed.

"I was just trying to decide if I find you sexier in your bra and panties or just totally naked."

She rolled her eyes at him. "You'll never change. So what's in the bag?" she asked, her curiosity getting the best of her.

"Alright, I'll show you but you have to close your eyes."

"Why?"

"Babe just do it." He waited until they were closed and took the item from the bag and opened it. "OK, you can open your eyes now."

She stared down at the diamond ring sitting in black velvet and gasped. "Oh my God, it's so beautiful," she said, looking at him, her eyes filled with tears. "When did this happen?" you get

He took the ring from the box and took her hand and placed it on her finger. He held her hand as he looked at it. "I bought it at the same time I bought you the earrings. I was planning on waiting until all the trouble was dealt with. I had planned on asking you for a romantic candlelit dinner somewhere special. But after what happened, knowing how fast life could be taken away, I couldn't wait to ask you to marry me so I proposed to you in the hospital."

"Oh Neil, it doesn't matter to me how or where you proposed, I'm just so happy that you did. I love you with all my heart."

He pushed her down onto the bed and climbed on top of her, she put her hands on his chest to stop him when he started kissing her. "Neil, you can't, you're not strong enough."

He stared deep into her eyes, he wanted her so bad, his cock was aching. "Please don't stop me. I promise to take it slow and easy, but I really need this, I need you."

She heard the urgency in his voice and the wanting in his eyes, she too wanted to feel him inside her. Cupping the back of his head she drew him down for a kiss. He had removed her bra and slid her panties down before entering her. He moved slowly up and down inside her as he kissed her passionately. He was true to his word, he took it slow and easy, making sure not to overexert himself. It was still amazing, both coming to a climax with an amazing orgasm for both of them.

"Damn, that was great," he said as he rolled off her. As great as it was, it did take a lot out of him, he was out of breath.

"It really was but I'm a little worried about you."

"Why?" he asked, feeling a little less like a man.

She noticed the look on his face and sensed what he was feeling. "You just had a major operation and maybe making love was a mistake. Don't get me wrong, it was amazing but until you are fully healed no more sex. Please don't be mad at me."

"Mad at you never, it's me that I'm mad at. I should have given you more, satisfied you better."

"What are you talking about? You did, it was even more beautiful and special. You took your time and made me feel loved. You don't always have to go all caveman when you make love to me. It was tender and sweet, only a real man can make a woman feel the way you just made me feel."

He drew her close, loving her all that much more. "Well, you are right, I should wait until I'm fully healed. I love you."

For the next week and a half, she catered to him, changed his bandage, and helped him to shower. That was the hardest part for them, showering together and not making love. His family came over for dinner one night, she felt it would cheer him up to see his niece.

"Oh wow, look at this ring, it's so beautiful," Judy said as she gushed over it. "Have you two set a date yet?"

Neil and Kiara looked at each other.

"Not yet, but I'd like to get married as soon as possible," he said, taking Kiara's hand and kissing it. "We'll discuss it later and get back to you."

Chrissy went over and pushed her way in between them, looking at Kiara's stomach. "Mommy says you have a baby in your tummy."

"That's right," she answered, smiling at the little girl.

"How did it get in there?"

Both Neil and Roy sat there with a grin on their faces, each wondering how the women were going to explain this to Chrissy.

Kiara was stunned, she didn't know what to say so she looked at Judy for help.

"Chrissy, why don't you draw Kiara a picture before we leave?" It worked every time, her little girl loved to draw and she jumped off the sofa and going to her backpack pulled out her paper and crayons.

"Well, we dodged a bullet this time. Now when you two decide on a date I'd love to help with the planning and I'll take you shopping for a wedding dress," Judy said, smiling at Kiara.

Later that night she reached her arm over to his side of the bed and found he wasn't in bed. Getting up she puts on her robe and goes to see where he had gotten to. She found him out on the balcony, leaning over the railing and just staring into space.

"Neil, what's wrong?" she asked, placing her hand on his shoulder.

He turned to give her a weak smile before turning back to stare out over the city. “I couldn't sleep. I've tried to forget what Eric had done but no matter how hard I try to push it from my mind it just keeps coming back to haunt me."

"I know how much you loved him and I believe he loved you too."

"I trusted him and he tried to kill me and he was going to kill you. I keep thinking if only I had known how unhappy he was I might have been able to help him. Is there no one that can be trusted?"

"You can trust me," she said, almost in tears.

He turned, putting his hands on her waist drew her closer. "Oh baby, you are the only one I know I can trust. Let's not wait to get married, let's do it right away."

"I'm all for that, when were you thinking of?"

"Two months from now, that should be plenty of time to plan a quick wedding and I'm going to take you back to Italy for a three-week honeymoon."

She smiled, putting her arms around his neck. "Then I better call Judy and get started on the plans. I'd like to get married in a church if that's alright with you?"

"Anything you want sweetheart, I just want you to be happy."

"When I was a little girl I dreamed of getting married in a church wearing a beautiful white dress. I never thought it would ever happen to me."

He pulled her closer. "My doctor's appointment is tomorrow but I'm feeling really good, better than ever. What say I take you back to bed and give you the full caveman experience? But I have to warn you, this cute little silk nightgown you have on is going to be laying in shreds at the bottom of the bed."

Before she could stop him he picked her up and tossed her like a sack of potatoes over his shoulder and carried her back to bed with her squealing loudly in his ears. True to his word he tore her nightgown off and pushed her back onto the bed. There was no going slow and easy, instead, he was like a wild animal in heat as he ravished every inch of her, making her scream as she reached several orgasms throughout the night. She smiled when he was finally finished with her, he was indeed back to his old self, even more than before.

"Hot damn, I'm back baby," he said as he pressed his lips against hers in a hot, passionate kiss. He then rolled off her, pulling her into his arms and his hand went to her stomach. "It's time for you to go back for a check-up, and this time I'm going with you. I'm never going to miss another one of your appointments."

"I wonder if we should learn the sex or just wait to be surprised," she said, placing her hand over his.

"It's up to you but I have a feeling it's going to be a girl."

"She smiled up at him. "It could be a boy you know."

He turned serious when he looked back at her. "I don't care whether it's a boy or girl, it's our baby so no matter what it is going to be it will be the most special baby ever born. Have I told you lately how much I love you?"

"Yes, all the time but I don't mind hearing it again."

"I love you," he said, lifting her head and kissing her.

She went with him the next day to his appointment and he was given a clean bill of health. Neil also had the doctor check her out and she too was fine as was the baby, she was then set up with a family doctor who would be delivering her baby. After the appointments were set up he took her out to lunch. It was so great being able to come and go without the worry of someone out to hurt them.

He had gone back to work, she started doing her online classes and along with Judy, they started organizing the wedding. The only cloud hanging over her head was when the time would come for her to go to court and testify about what happened and what she saw when she was held captive and used as a Sex Kitten. She wasn't looking forward to seeing Charlie again, it hurt too much remembering what he had done to her.

Judy took her shopping for the perfect dress and as Chrissy was the flower girl she went so that she could get a new dress. Kiara found the one she fell in love with, she liked that it was shaped to hide the baby bump that was starting to grow. They stopped to have lunch before going back to Judy's where she planned on meeting Neil.

She found it strange that Chrissy was acting weird, she was so hyper, jumping around, and kept asking when they could go home. This was so unlike her, usually, she wanted to go to the park or shop more.

"Oh don't mind her, she's just excited about being the flower girl at your wedding," Judy said as she looked at her daughter and shook her head.

"Mommy, is it time yet, can we go home now?"

"Not yet, baby, but soon."

"But we can't be late for the surprise."

"Surprise, what surprise?" Kiara asked, looking at both of them.

Judy laughed nervously. “Oh, it's nothing really. Roy said he had something for her, you know how kids are. But it is getting late so maybe we should head home now."

"Just let me use the lady's room before we leave, ever since I became pregnant I need to pee a lot."

When Kiara left the table Judy pulled Chrissy over to her. "Honey, you almost gave away the surprise, now don't say anything else, OK?"

"OK, mommy."

"That's ok baby. Here she comes, now remember, not a word."

Chrissy used her little fingers to make a zipper motion across her lips.

Kiara walked back over to them, she had a feeling they were up to something when she saw them whispering and saw the little girl when she ran her fingers over her lips.

Chapter 15

When they got to Judy's place and the car was put into park Chrissy got out, taking Kiara's hand she started dragging her to the door and inside. "Come on Aunt Kiara, hurry up," she said with the excitement of a child her age.

As soon as she stepped inside both Neil and Roy shouted in surprise. She looked around the room and saw the balloons, birthday decorations, and a cake sitting on the coffee table along with some wrapped gifts. Her eyes teared up and she looked over at Neil. She was speechless and wondered how they knew today was her birthday, she hadn't told anyone, not even the man she was marrying.

Neil went over, putting his arms around her. "Happy Birthday baby."

She looked up at him. "How did you know?" she asked, her eyes glistening with tears.

He chuckled. "When you went and got all your paperwork for a new birth certificate and social security number that's when I saw your birth date. Are you surprised?"

She nodded and looked at the others. "Thank you all so much. I've never celebrated my birthday before and this is a wonderful surprise." She buried her face in his chest, too choked up to say anything else.

He held her in his arms, looking over at the others. They stayed that way for only a few seconds before Chrissy broke them up.

"Come on Aunt Kiara, blow out your candles so then you can open your presents."

With his arm around her waist, he walked her over to the sofa where she sat down and looked at the cake. "What a beautiful cake," she said before blowing out the candles.

Once she did Chrissy handed her one of the presents. "This is from mommy and daddy."

She took the gift, her heart was racing, and started tearing off the wrapper while the others watched with smiles on their faces. It was a pink cashmere sweater. "Oh this is so beautiful, thank you so much," she said, looking at them with tears in her eyes as she rubbed the material over her cheek, loving the feel of it.

"This one is from me," Chrissy said, handing her a small box.

"Opening it she pulled the little girl in for a hug. "I love it, thank you, sweetheart." It was a matching cashmere scarf to go with the sweater and a small black wallet. "You all shouldn't have, but thank you so much, I love the gifts."

"There's some from Uncle Neil," Chrissy said, handing her a box wrapped in pink paper.

Kiara was pleasantly shocked and surprised when she pulled out a black Saint Laurent Cabas purse. "Oh Neil, you shouldn't have." She knew that the bag was really expensive and she felt overwhelmed.

He sat down next to her. "If you don't like it you can return it and get the one you want."

"No," she said, shaking her head. “I love it, thank you," she said, reaching over and she kissed him on the lips.

"There's one more for you from Uncle Neil," Chrissy said, pulling a smaller box from under the table and handing it to her.

"You've already given me so much."

"Open it," he said, grinning.

With hands that shook she opened it, it was a new phone, not just any phone, but the top of the line. "I love it," she said, choking back a sob.

He put his arm around her shoulder. "There's a place inside the purse for you to put it in. See if it'll fit." He sat anxiously waiting for her to see what was inside.

She opened the purse and found another small wrapped gift inside. "What's this?" she asked, looking at him.

"Open it and find out." It gave him so much pleasure spoiling her, his heart felt so warm and full of love.

The tears flowed when she saw the diamond necklace. It was all too much for her, excusing herself she laid it down and getting up went into the kitchen. She heard footsteps approaching and knew it was Neil, she felt his hands on her shoulders when he turned her around to face him.

"What's wrong?" he asked, looking at her with concern when he saw she was crying.

"Don't get me wrong, I love all the gifts and I love you. I'm not used to getting gifts, especially ones so expensive. I don't want you to think you have to buy me things. You're paying for everything, the wedding, the honeymoon. I've got nothing to give you."

He gave her a little shake, looking deep into her eyes. "Are you crazy? You've given me so much already, your love and the best gift ever which is priceless." He placed his hand over her stomach. "You are giving me the best gift ever, our baby." He turned her around and placed the necklace around her neck. “I hope you like this, I tried finding one that would match your earrings, and this was the best I could find."

"This is perfect, I love it, thank you."

"Let's get one thing straight, you're going to be my wife so what is mine will also be yours and I plan on spoiling you. I hope you can live with that." He pulled her roughly into his arms, his lips came crashing down on hers in a long, passionate kiss.

"Oh, that's so gross."

They stopped kissing when they heard what Chrissy said, looking at each other they laughed and moved from their embrace.

"Come cut the cake Aunt Kiara, I want cake and ice cream," she said, taking her hand and pulling her into the living room.

Walking hand in hand they went with her back into the living room where Kiara started cutting it into slices, giving Chrissy the first piece.

For the next couple of hours, they sat around, talking about the wedding plans. Neil and Roy went outside and sat down drinking beer while the woman gave Chrissy her bath and got her ready for bed, she went and kissed the guys before going back inside and getting into bed.

The women went and joined the men, and Kiara sat on Neil's lap. "I really want to thank you all for the party and gifts."

"Well, my big brother told us you never had a birthday party or gifts so we all decided to throw a small one. Chrissy almost spilled the beans earlier."

"I thought you two were acting a bit strange all day," she said, smiling. She had put on the sweater she received and kept touching it. "I just love this, it's so soft, I've never had anything like it before."

"I like things that are soft too," Neil said, putting his hand on her leg and starting moving it up.

Blushing, she grabbed his hand before he got too far up her leg. "Behave yourself." She was embarrassed when he did that in front of his family. She thought they would be appalled but glancing over at them she saw that they were grinning.

An hour later she put her arms around his neck. "I'm getting tired, can we go home soon?"

He loved it when she gave him those puppy eyes of hers and she did look tired. "Yes, it is getting late and you've had a busy day."

They gathered up her gifts along with a huge slice of the birthday cake and saying their goodbyes they headed home. There she went right to the bedroom to get ready for bed, nightgown on. She was standing in front of the mirror taking off her necklace when she saw him approaching and felt his arms going around her waist and his lips going to her neck.

"I can't wait until we are married, I love you so much," he said, kissing her neck and letting his hand slide down her body. He lifted her gown up and put his hand inside her panties and started rubbing his fingers against her feminine folds. She was already wet for him and when she started moaning he turned her around, sliding the straps of her gown down past her shoulders. He moved his lips down her neck and over her soft shoulder to her breasts. Picking her up into his arms he carried her over to the bed.

As she sat on the edge of the bed she started unbuckling his pants and pulled them down along with his briefs. She licked her lips seductively when she saw his erection. "I see you have another birthday present for me."

He smiled as he lowered her down onto the bed. "It's more of a gift for me."

Two hours later they both lay on their backs, exhausted and out of breath.

"Happy Birthday baby," he said, taking her hand in his.

It was the middle of the night when he woke up and she wasn't in bed. It wasn't like her to wake up through the night so being worried he went to find her. He saw the light in the kitchen was on so he headed there, stopping in the doorway. There she was with a guilty look and icing on her face when she saw him.

"I had a craving for something sweet," she said, fork in hand with the cake in front of her.

Smirking, he walked over to the drawer and took out a fork, and sat across from her. He took a forkful of cake. "I did too, but since I already had it earlier I'll have some cake too."

"Neil, I want us to always be honest with each other. I've known so many people who have kept things from their partners and when it comes out it never ends well. No matter what it is, I want you to tell me, even if I might get mad."

"I totally agree with you. Also, let's never go to bed angry and always kiss goodnight and say we love each other. I think this was the secret to my parent's marriage and I'd like for us to have a marriage like theirs, built on a foundation of love and trust."

She pushed the cake away. "I have to stop eating like this or I'll get as big as a horse."

"You're eating for two," he said, setting his fork down. "You're so beautiful and it's I who needs to watch my weight. I need to keep this body in shape for my young wife."

"It's not your body I love, it's you," she said, getting up and going over and sitting on his lap she put her arms around his neck.

"This scar on my chest, does it not turn you off?"

She traced the scar with the tips of her fingers. "No, I wouldn't care if you were covered in scars, I would still love you no matter what. Don't ever doubt my love for you."

"Let's go back to bed," he said, lifting her up and carrying her back to bed.

She put her arms around his neck, she loved it whenever he carried her to bed. There was something hot about a man who had no trouble carrying a woman, it turned her on, making her want him.

The next few weeks were busy ones, the church was booked, the hall for the reception was and everyone had their outfits. Neil had booked the same suite in Italy where they had stayed when they were there last time. Roy was going to be Neil's best man, Judy was the maid of honor, and of course, Chrissy was the flower girl. Roy's partner William was going to walk Kiara down the aisle.

The morning of the wedding she woke up in a strange bed, having stayed the night at Judy's place while Roy stayed at Neil's. They both wanted to follow some wedding traditions, and not seeing the bride the night before the wedding was one of them.

Chrissy peeked her head inside the door. "Are you awake, Aunt Kiara?"

She sat up, rubbing the sleep from her eyes. "I'm awake honey."

Chrissy ran over and jumped on the bed. "Mommy says to get you to come down and eat breakfast before the lady comes to do our hair. I'm getting mine done too and mommy says I can wear some of her perfume, she never lets me wear it."

After they ate she took a nice relaxing bath, she was missing Neil and hoped he and Roy didn't drink too much last night. She couldn't wait to be standing at the front of the church with him and for the moment they were pronounced man and wife.

Three women showed up a little later to do all their hair and make-up, once that was done it was time to put on their dresses. Kiara was just about to put on the necklace when Judy walked in.

"Oh my, you look so beautiful."

"Thank you. I'm a little nervous and not sure if I can get my necklace up, would you help me?"

"Turn around," she said, taking the necklace from her. "I want you to know I've never seen my brother this happy. I was beginning to think he would never find someone to love. You're good for him and I know you both will have a happy marriage. I've always wanted a sister and now I have one."

They were hugging when Chrissy ran in wearing her dress. "Mommy, look at me, don't I look pretty?"

"Oh, you sure do baby girl."

"Aunt Kiara, you look pretty too," she said, giving her a hug.

Kiara kneeled down to her level. "You are going to be the prettiest girl at the wedding. Are you ready to toss the petals when you go down the aisle?"

"Yes, can we go now?"

Judy laughed. "We should get ready to leave for the church. If we're late Neil will have a nervous breakdown."

Neil and Roy got to the church and went into the back room to wait for the service to start. He was pacing back and forth until Roy went over to strengthen his tie. "Relax man, it won't be long now."

He took a deep breath. "So have you got any words of wisdom for a man who is about to get married?"

"Actually I do. The recipe for a successful marriage is trust and forgiveness. But the most important thing is when your wife talks to you, you listen to her. I mean really listen, just don't pretend to. If another woman comes onto you, don't act on it. It might be tempting but just remember why you got married and know you could lose the most important person in your life."

"I would never cheat on Kiara."

"I know that, but some women won't care if you're married, they will try and take what belongs to another. Just keep on telling Kiara how much you love her, especially during her pregnancy. When the mood swings come, they will just be patient with her." He gave him a light tap on his cheek. "It's about to start, are you ready to go out front now?"

"Damn straight I am," he answered back, doing up the buttons on his jacket.

The wedding music started playing and the guys looked at each other and smiled when they saw Chrissy walking towards them. Her face was beaming as she dropped a few rose petals as she made her way toward them. Then Roy gave Judy a big smile when he saw her, he thought she was even more beautiful today than the first day he had laid eyes on her.

Then when Kiara made her appearance Neil couldn't take his eyes off her. He had to wonder if it was all a dream as she made her way to him, their eyes locked. He could feel his hands trembling, his heart beating fast, she looked like an angel, her beauty took his breath away. The money he spent on this wedding was worth every penny and he'd do it again in a heartbeat. When she got to him he took her hands in his when she handed her bouquet of flowers to Judy.

"You're beautiful," he said, wanting so badly to take her in his arms. **********

As soon as she saw him standing at the front of the church she wanted to cry, he looked so handsome in his suit and she couldn't believe how lucky she was to find a man like him. She loved him so much and when she took his hands she wasn't sure if it was his or her hands that were trembling. She stared into his eyes during the whole ceremony and once the minister pronounced them man and wife she put her arms around him when he pulled her in for a kiss.

They didn't get much time to talk when they got outside, what with everyone gathered around them, wishing them all the best, Then they walked around the corner to where they had booked the hall for their dinner and reception. He held her hand and kept looking at her, smiling and telling her how much he loved her.

A sit-down four-course meal was served, and everyone kept tapping their glass to get the couple to kiss, which they didn't mind. With the meal done with the cake cut and served it was time for the first dance.

He took her hand and led her onto the dance floor, pulling her into his arms. "We haven't had much time to talk and I've been dying to tell you something."

"What's that?" she asked, looking up at him with so much love.

"First, I want to tell you how much I love this dress, you look stunning. I also want to tell you how much I love you and that I'm so glad I found you on that site. You've changed my life for the better, you are my whole life now. I promise to always love you, to give you the life you deserve."

She started to tear up. "I love you too, and all I want is you, now and forever." She lifted her head up and kissed him.

Neil made sure to have a couple of dances with Chrissy, telling her she was so pretty in her new dress and told her what a great job she did being the flower girl. It was starting to get late, Roy and Judy had taken their daughter home so Neil figured it was a good time for them to head back to their place. She was starting to get tired and they had to be up early to catch their flight to Italy.

Back at his suite, he turned on some romantic music, taking her in his arms and they started dancing, their bodies moving in perfect harmony.

"This has been the most perfect day ever, you really went all out," she said, resting her head on his shoulder. "The flowers, church, and everything else, I felt like Cinderella. It was all so wonderful, thank you for a night that I'll remember for the rest of my life."

"I can't change what happened to you in the past but I can make your future brighter. I'm going to make sure you never hurt again. Now, let's get you out of this dress, it's time to make love as husband and wife."

Later on in Italy: She lay in his arms, holding her hand out to look at her wedding rings. "You have such amazing taste. I sometimes wonder if this is all a dream."

"It's not a dream sweetheart. I thought after breakfast we could go sightseeing and then tonight we could go see the ballet. Seeing we have three weeks here we can take our time doing whatever you want. Now that you're pregnant I don't want you overdoing it."

On their next week in Italy, he took her to the opera, they had balcony seats. Halfway through it, she happened to turn her head, and on the next balcony were Steven and Pauline Driver. Putting her hand on Neil's arm she leaned over to whisper in his ear. "That Steven guy is on the next balcony to ours."

He looked over at the exact time Steven glanced their way. "Just our luck to find him here when we're on our honeymoon. We'll just ignore him and if he tries to talk to you he'll find himself flat on his ass."

By the end of the show, they had hoped to avoid Steven but as luck would have it Pauline spotted them and called out, dragging Steven with her.

"Neil, it's so nice to see you again. I can't believe we're all here again and Miss Finn it's so lovely to see you again."

Taking Kiara's hand held it up. "Actually it's Mrs. Hicks now, we're married." He looked at Steven and could see the man starting to sweat as he looked everywhere but at them.

"Oh that's great news, isn't it Steven?"

Steven cleared his throat, still not looking at them. "Yes, yes, just wonderful."

Pauline gave them both a hug. "Let us take you out for a drink and we can catch up." She looked at Kiara's baby bump and smiled. "Oh, you're expecting, that's wonderful. We also heard that you had been shot and about those poor women, that was so horrible but we are happy to see that you are Ok."

Neil had always liked the woman and it was obvious that she still had no idea that her husband was a pervert that had used that site on several occasions. Oh, how he wanted to tell her but knew it really was none of his business. "We would love to join you but we are on our honeymoon and Kiara is tired. But it was lovely seeing you again, take care." Without saying anything to Steven he put his arm around her waist and they left the building.

"Did you notice how Steven wouldn't even look at us?" she asked as she got ready for bed that night.

"He was afraid to?"

"Why would he be afraid?"

"Because the last time I saw him I showed him a preview of what would happen to him if he ever so much as glanced in your direction. I don't want to talk about him, let's just go to bed, I'm horny and want to be inside your hot pussy."

"You're horrible," she said, laughing when he picked her up and carried her over to the bed.

After three amazing weeks in Italy, it was time to go back home. They had so much to do when they got back. He had his business to take care of and she had her online classes to catch up on, not to mention getting ready for the baby to come.

Once home she flopped down onto their bed. "I'm so tired, all I want to do is go right to sleep," she said, yawning.

He had noticed that in the last couple of days she got tired a lot and was suffering from heartburn. It worried him so he checked on the internet and learned that it was normal for some women. It had mentioned that it could mean that the baby was going to have lots of hair when he or she was born. Still, he was going to have the doctor check her out.

He made a doctor's appointment for her two days after they arrived home. It was time for a scan and they sat in the room waiting for the doctor to come in.

"So you still want to wait and be surprised about the sex?" he asked, standing by her side as he held her hand.

"Yes," she replied just as the doctor came in and got started.

They stared at the screen when he ran the wand over her stomach. "Well now, how did I miss this the first time?"

"Is something wrong?" Neil asked, his face turning pale.

"That depends on you I guess. But it appears as if you are having twins, this is a good surprise right?"

"Twins," she said, looking at Neil they both broke out in a smile,

Before leaving the doctor's office he gave her something for the heartburn since it was so bad that it had been making her sick. He also told her she had to take it easy and get lots of rest.

"Wow, just wait until we tell the others we're having twins," Neil said beaming.

EPILOGUE

Neil was thrilled when they were told she was carrying twins, it explained why she was always so tired. When they were alone she started crying, and he went and put his arms around her, he was confused, he thought she would have been happy. "Honey, are you not happy to be having twins?"

"It's not that, these are happy tears. I wanted more than one but I wasn't expecting to have two at once. My life is so amazing, I have you and now two babies. I grew up having to take care of myself, never knowing a mother's love. Our children will be loved and taken care of and the best part is they will have a sibling to grow up with." She put her arms around his neck. "I love you so much."

Since she was hungry he took her to lunch then later when they got home she went to take a nap. He decided to call Judy and tell her the good news, she was tickled pink and couldn't stop yelping for joy.

"Twins, now you make sure she gets plenty of rest and don't be letting her do so much housework. You hire someone to do it, and I'll come over in a few days and bring some baby books, you're going to need to start buying cribs and everything they will need. I have to phone Roy and tell him the good news," she said and hung up.

The following week he said he wanted to take her for a short drive, that he had something to show her. She kept trying to get him to tell her but he said it was a surprise. After driving for twenty minutes he stopped in front of a house that had a for sale sign on it.

She turned her head and looked out the window at the house. "What are we doing here?"

He undid his seatbelt and leaning over put his arm around her shoulders. "Ever since we found out you were having twins I started thinking about things. We need a proper home to raise our children, not in a hotel. I remember that first night we went to dinner at my sister's place and you said you would love to live in a house like that someday."

"You remember me saying that?"

"I always listen to you when you talk. I started looking through the real estate listings and came across this property. It has four bedrooms, four bathrooms, a large kitchen, and a dining room. A huge living room with a fireplace, an office and there's even a spare room on the main floor that can be used as a playroom for the kids. Oh, and there's a great backyard too. I thought we could go in and take a look."

"But it looks so expensive."

"Baby, stop worrying about it, you know we can afford it. So how about it, you want to go in and take a look?"

She couldn't stop smiling. "Yes, since we're here we might as well."

They both fell in love with it the moment they walked in the front door and even more so as they went from room to room. Standing in the master bedroom after checking the ensuite he pulled her into his arms.

"I can see us making mad, passionate love in this room every night. But if you want to keep looking at other houses we can, but I really think this is the perfect house for us."

"I love it," she said, shedding more tears. "I don't need to see any more houses, this one feels like home to me." She threw her arms around him, her lips went to his mouth and she gave him a long, passionate kiss.

That night his family came over for dinner, she had made Chrissy's favorite meal, spaghetti and chocolate cake for dessert. That night they told them about the house Neil was buying and that they would be moving into it a month from today.

With dinner over, the guys talked, Chrissy played with her new toy that Neil had bought her and the women went through the baby books, picking out everything for the babies. The guys took their beers into the kitchen and sat down to talk.

"Wow, twins," Roy said, smiling as he shook his head. "That's going to be a handful, there goes your sex life."

"What are you talking about?"

"All I'm saying is that when a woman has a baby, what with the overnight feedings she's going to be too tired to have sex. I can't imagine what it's going to be like having twins. Be prepared to take lots of cold showers."

"No, it won't be like that with us." He hadn't given her being too tired for sex after the baby was born any thought until now. Then he smiled at Roy. "I'm not worried, she likes it as much as I do and I'll be riding her plenty."

"Riding who?" Judy's voice bellowed out as she walked over to them.

"Nothing, we were just kidding around," he said, winking at his sister.

"I just bet you were," she answered, giving him a swat upside the head before looking at Roy. "Chrissy's asleep so we better go home now, you'll have to carry her."

That night in bed they went through books, picking out furniture for their new home. He wanted to have everything bought and placed before they moved in. With her carrying twins and being tired he wanted to take the burden off her shoulders. All she had to do was choose what she liked and he would take care of the rest. What Roy had said was weighing on his mind so he thought he would bring it up.

"So, Roy was telling me that after Judy had Chrissy she was always tired. What with the night feedings and taking care of her that their sex life suffered for a long time."

She looked up at him and smiled. "So you think with us having twins I might not want you anymore."

"I know for the first while you'll be too tired." He sat up to look her in the eyes. "I'm just saying I find you so hot and I won't rush you into it until you're ready, no matter how long it takes. It's not going to be easy because I want you all the time."

She pushed him down and got on top of him, smiling. "You have nothing to worry about, I love your anaconda and I'll be wanting it all the time. Maybe not the first couple of weeks or so but after that, watch out. Make sure you get lots of rest because you're going to need it," she said before lowering her head to kiss him.

A month later they moved into their home, Neil's family came over bringing dinner and a housewarming gift, and some things for the babies. Chrissy ran from room to room, exploring. The cribs had arrived and the guys set them up while the women talked and heated up the meal.

"Kiara looks really happy, she loves this house, you did good Neil. I almost forgot to tell you, she won't have to testify against Charlie. We have enough pieces of evidence against him along with the written statement she made a while back. As she had no idea he was involved there was no reason for her to face him in court. It's all over, now you both can relax and move on with your life."

"That's a relief, I didn't want her to have to go through all that stress, not in her condition."

Before Judy and Roy were leaving to go home Kiara wanted the furniture in the living room moved, she wasn't happy with where the movers had put it. After several times the guys breathed a sigh of relief when she finally settled on where she wanted it.

"Wait, I think the sofa should be over there," she points out. "The chair would look better by the fireplace."

Neil was sweating, he was slowly losing his patience. "Babe, this is the fourth time we've moved the furniture. It's fine where it is."

Tears sprang to her eyes, this was the first time he had spoken so harshly to her. She turned and walked away, going into the kitchen. She heard someone enter and knew it was him by his scent and she started sniffling. "I'm sorry for being such a pain."

He felt like hell for snapping at her, going over he put his arms around her. "No, I'm the one who's sorry, I shouldn't have snapped at you. Come on, let's go move the furniture," he said, giving her a kiss.

When they got back to the living room they found that Roy and Judy had already moved it. "Kiara was right, it does look better here," she said, smiling at them.

That night when they got into bed she snuggled up to him. "Our first night in our new home, I think we should christen the bed," she said, her hand going down to his crotch. "Unless you don't fancy making love to a pregnant woman."

He pushed her down and got on top. "What do you think?" he asked, his lips going to hers.

Kiara was now eight months pregnant when she went into labor, waking him up in the middle of the night. They were told that it was common for a woman to give birth a month early, especially when having twins so they weren't too worried about it.

He called his sister when they got to the hospital and before she was taken into the room. "This is it, sweetheart, it won't be long now. I want you to know how much I love you."

She held his hand. "I love you too and you have made me so happy. You are going to be a great dad."

"Do you really think so?"

"I've watched you with Chrissy, the way you treat her, and how much you love her. If you can be that way with your niece just imagine how you will be with your own children."

Judy and Roy showed up, going over and giving her a hug and kiss. "It won't be long until you're holding those precious babies in your arms," she said, going over to hug Neil.

For over an hour they chatted, looking at the outfits Judy had brought for the babies when Kiara gripped Neil's hand. "You better call the doctor, it's time."

They were taken into the delivery room and in just a few short hours she gave birth to two baby boys, both small, weighing under six pounds and with a full head of hair.

"Oh my, they are so beautiful," Judy said as she gushed over them when they were allowed to go see her and the babies. "What are their names?"

"The one with the dark hair is Simon, the blond is Shawn," both Neil and Kiara said at the same time.

"They're so small, Chrissy can't wait to meet her cousins," Roy said as he looked down at the two babies, both were fast asleep.

Seven weeks later Judy and Chrissy came over to visit Kiara and the twins, she adored her cousins.

She sat by their cribs reading a story to them while her mother and aunt were talking.

"Is everything alright?" Judy asked her when she noticed she looked sad.

"It's Neil, he hasn't tried to touch me since before the twins were born. I think he feels it's too soon but Judy, I'm more than ready. What should I do?"

"Tell you what, go upstairs, take off all your clothes and put on a coat, then go visit him at work. Show that man you are more than ready. Chrissy and I will watch the twins."

"Are you sure?" she asked, feeling a little shy about doing what she suggested.

"Yes, now get going."

Kiara took a cab to the hotel and went looking for him, she was told he was in his office.

When he saw her he stood up. "This is a nice surprise, but where are the babies?"

"Judy's watching them." She locked the door and saw the look of confusion on his face. "I've waited long enough for you to make the first move so I will." She dropped her coat, showing him her full nakedness.

His eyes grew wide as he looked her over from head to toe and back again. "Holy shit, you have no idea how much I've been wanting you," he said, removing his clothes and taking a hold of her, drawing her into his arms and kissing her. He walked her back to the sofa and lowered her down. He ignored the ringing of the phone as they kissed and groped each other for a good twenty minutes. He muffled her screams with his kiss when he started thrusting inside her, bringing them both to a long-needed orgasm.

She ran her hands down his back. "Neil, that was amazing but we shouldn't have waited so long to do this."

"Baby, I didn't want to wait this long but I didn't know if you were ready."

"Oh, I'm ready."

He smiled at her, kissing her again. “Yes, you've made it crystal clear, I love you so much," he said, taking her once again before they left to go back home.

To sum things up once the twins started school Kiara went to work alongside Neil, he made her partner in the business. They didn't have any more children, but it wasn't due to a lack of trying. They stayed deeply in love and their passion grew more passionate. She remained affectionate toward him, cuddling up to him like a soft little kitten.

The end:

www.ingramcontent.com/pod-product-compliance
Lightning Source LLC
LaVergne TN
LVHW010542160826
845677LV00013B/2973
* 9 7 9 8 3 6 1 1 7 3 2 5 9 *